THE SECRETS

***Two brothers a...
separated at bi...***

Nico—...

Brought up to ... Greek boy,
he's always felt like an outsider. He's turned his back
on his parents' fortune to become one of Xanos'
most powerful exports.

Nothing will stand in the way of him discovering
the truth—until he stumbles upon a virgin bride…
an encounter that has shameful consequences…

Zander—the forgotten twin

He took his chances on the streets rather than
spend another moment under his cruel father's roof.
He's pulled himself up by the bootstraps and is
unrivalled in business—and the bedroom!

He wants the best people around him, and
Charlotte is the best PA! But she works for his rival…
unless he can tempt her over to the dark side…

Look out for Zander's story
AN INDECENT PROPOSITION
Coming soon!

'I will not be your long-time lover. I am no one's escape…' He saw her eyes shutter. **'But I will be with you tonight.'**

'Just tonight?' She wanted more than that.

'Only tonight…' He looked at her, his eyes roaming the body he had been thinking about for hours now. A virgin bride, who would stay that way if not for him. 'You come to my bed. I will show you all you miss out on if you choose to live this lie…'

'I have no choice.'

'Always we have choices,' Nico said, and this was his—to choose not to examine his feelings tonight. His mind was black and here was light. The streets of Xanos had unsettled him, stirred emotions that he sorely wanted gone. He wanted diversion and here it had been delivered to him—in the shape of a tear-streaked, beautiful virgin.

A SHAMEFUL CONSEQUENCE

BY
CAROL MARINELLI

First published in Great Britain 2011
by Mills & Boon, an imprint of Harlequin (UK) Limited,
Eton House, 18-24 Paradise Road, Richmond, Surrey TW9 1SR

© Carol Marinelli 2011

ISBN: 978 0 263 88703 7

Harlequin (UK) policy is to use papers that are natural, renewable and recyclable products and made from wood grown in sustainable forests. The logging and manufacturing process conform to the legal environmental regulations of the country of origin.

Printed and bound in Spain
by Blackprint CPI, Barcelona

Carol Marinelli recently filled in a form where she was asked for her job title and was thrilled, after all these years, to be able to put down her answer as 'writer'.

Then it asked what Carol did for relaxation and, after chewing her pen for a moment, Carol put down the truth—'writing'. The third question asked, 'What are your hobbies?' Well, not wanting to look obsessed or, worse still, boring, she crossed the fingers on her free hand and answered 'swimming and tennis'. But, given that the chlorine in the pool does terrible things to her highlights, and the closest she's got to a tennis racket in the last couple of years is watching the Australian Open, I'm sure you can guess the real answer!

Recent titles by the same author:

HEART OF THE DESERT
THE DEVIL WEARS KOLOVSKY

**Carol also writes for
Mills & Boon® Medical™ Romance!**

**Did you know these are also available as eBooks?
Visit www.millsandboon.co.uk**

PROLOGUE

'Tonight they have their own rooms,' Alexandros said. 'Separate rooms.'

'What harm…?' Roula started and then stopped— she had learnt not to question Alexandros's decisions, but on this one she had to stand up to him. It would be cruel to separate the babies, so she tried another route. 'They will wake you with their tears.'

'Let them cry—that is the way they will learn that at night you are with me.' He ran a hand between her thighs, told her that tonight there would be no excuses, not that he listened when she made them.

Her only relief was the slam of the door when he left to spend the day sitting outside the taverna, playing cards and drinking, but Roula's relief lasted just a moment before the countdown started—dreading his return.

Seventeen and the mother of twins, they were her only shining light. More beautiful than any other babies, she could watch them sleep for hours, the little snubs of their noses, pushed up by their fingers as they sucked on their thumbs, eyelashes so long that they met the curve of their cheeks. Sometimes one would open his eyes to look at the other. Huge black eyes would gaze at his brother, soothed by what he saw, and then close again.

Mirror image twins, the midwife had told Roula when she'd delivered them. Identical, but opposite, one right handed the other left, their soft baby hair swirled to the right on Nico, to the left on little Alexandros.

At almost a year, still they shared a cot, screaming if she tried to separate them. Even if their cribs were pushed together, their protests would not abate. Now tonight he would force them into separate rooms.

And she would hear their screams all night as her husband used her body—and Roula could not take it any more.

Would not.

Her father would surely help if he knew. Alexandros did not like her to go out, so she had seen her father only a couple of times since her marriage—he had wanted her to marry, the little money he got for his paintings could not support them both. He had been a little eccentric since her mother's death; he preferred to be alone, but he would surely not want this life for his daughter and grandsons.

'Now,' she told herself, 'You must do it now.' She had maybe five or six hours before Alexandros would return. She ran down the hallway, pulled out a case and filled it with the few clothes she had for her babies, and then she ran into the kitchen to a jar she had hidden, filled with money she had been secretly hoarding for months now.

'This is how you repay me?' Roula froze when she heard his voice and then simply detached as he beat her, as he told her she was a thief to take from the man who put a roof over her head. 'You want to leave, then get out!' How her heart soared for a brief moment, but then Alexandros dealt his most brutal blow. 'You get half…' He hauled her to the bedroom where her babies lay screaming, woken by the terrible sounds. 'Which one is the firstborn?' He did not recognise his own sons. 'Which one is Alexandros?'

And when she answered he picked up the other babe and thrust Nico at her.

'Take him, and get out.'

She ran to her father's, clutching Nico. Terrified for Alexandros left alone with him, sure that her father would help her sort it out. Along the streets she ran, till finally home was in view, except it was boarded up. Her father was now dead, the disgusted neighbours told her, for she had neglected him in his final days and had not bothered to attend his funeral. The worst was finding out that her husband had been informed, had known, and not thought to tell her.

'We will get your brother back,' she said to a scream-ing Nico. The local policeman drank regularly with Alexandros so he would be no help, but she would go to the main town of Xanos, which was on the north of the island, to the lawyer that was there.

She took a ride on a truck and had to pay the driver

in the vilest of ways, but she did it for her son. She did it many times again when she found that the rich young lawyer wanted money upfront before helping her.

A little cheap ouzo from the lid meant Nico slept at night and she could earn more money. The rest of the bottle got her through.

And she tried.

Till one day, sitting holding her baby in an alleyway, she heard a man's voice.

'How much?'

Roula looked up and she was about to name her paltry fee, but there was a woman standing next to him, and that was one thing Roula would not do.

'I'm not interested.'

Except he did not want her body. 'How much for him?'

And he told her they were childless—that they were on holiday from the mainland to get over their grief. He told her about the money and education they could give her beautiful boy, that they would move to the neighbouring island of Lathira and would raise him as their own. She thought of Alexandros, who was still with that monster, and somehow she had to save him. She thought of the ouzo and the clients she would service tonight and all the terrible things she had done. Surely Nico deserved better.

Nico would settle, Roula told herself again as the couple left the rich lawyer's ofice with her baby. Soon Nico would forget.

She, on the other hand, would spend the rest of her life trying to.

CHAPTER ONE

PERHAPS he should have rung.

As the car swept into the drive of his parents' home, Nico Eliades questioned what he was even doing here—but a business deal in Athens had been closed earlier than expected, the hotel he had been intending to purchase was now his, and with a rare weekend free he had decided, given he was so close, to do his duty and fly to Lathira and visit his parents.

It did not feel like home.

Only duty led him up the steps.

Guilt even.

Because he did not like them. Did not like the way his parents used their wealth, and the way their egos required constant massage. His father had come from the mainland when Nico was one and had purchased two luxury boats that now cruised the Greek islands. No doubt, today, there would be another argument, another demand that he return to live here and invest some of his very considerable fortune in the family business. Another teary plea from his mother, to find a bride and give them grandchildren—that he should thank them for all they had done.

Thank them?

For what?

Nico blew out a breath because he did not want to go in there hostile, truly did not want another row, but always they threw in that line, always they told him he should be more grateful—for the schooling, for the clothing, for the chances.

For doing what any parent would surely do, could they afford it, for their son.

'They are not here.' The maid looked worried, for his parents would be angry they had missed a rare visit from Nico. 'They are at the wedding, they don't return till to-morrow.'

'Ah, the wedding.' Nico had forgotten. He had told his parents he would not be attending and for once they had not argued. It was the wedding of Stavros, the son of Dimitri, his father's main business rival. Normally at events such as these, his father insisted Nico attend because he wanted to parade his more successful son.

Nico's ego did not need it.

But, surprisingly, his parents had not pressed him to attend on this occasion.

Now here he was, reluctant to leave without having at least seen them—it had been weeks, no, months since he had been back, and if he saw them now then it could be several months more before he had to visit again.

'Where?' Nico asked the maid. 'Where is the wedding?'

Because Charlotte, his PA, had told him of the invitation, just not of the details.

'Xanos.' The maid said and screwed up her nose slightly as she did so, because even though Xanos had recently become the most exclusive retreat for the rich and famous, the locals were poor and the people of Lathira considered themselves superior. 'That is where the bride is from so they must marry there.'

'In the south?' Nico asked, because that would mean Stavros had done well for himself. But the maid gave a small smile as she answered.

'No, in the old town—your father and Dimitri have to rough it tonight.'

And now Nico did smile, for though his father was certainly wealthy, the south with its luxury resorts and exclusive access was way beyond his father's reach.

He would go, Nico decided.

He did not care that he had declined, details like that did not concern him. Staff moved mountains, tables appeared, presidential suites were conjured up wherever he landed—Charlotte would sort it out.

Except she, too, was at a wedding today in London, he remembered.

'Sort out my clothes,' he told the maid, as his driver brought up his cases and Nico told him to arrange the transport.

'The transport is all taken.' The driver was nervous to inform him. 'The helicopters took all the family last night, they don't return till tomorrow.'

'No problem.' Dressed and ready, he ordered the driver to the ferry. He was used to different drivers:

Nico did not really have a base. What he was not used to was attending to small details for himself, but his PA was usually available night and day and she did deserve this one weekend off.

He did not care for the stares of his fellow passengers as he paid for his ticket.

Dressed in a dark suit, he sat amongst tourists who gaped at the beautiful man in dark glasses, who did not belong on the local ferry.

Public transport was not so bad, Nico decided, buying a strong coffee, intending to read the paper to pass the time, but there was a baby crying behind him and it would not stop.

He tried to concentrate on the paper, but the baby's screams grew louder; there was a discomfort that spread through him, a growing unease as the ferry dipped and rose, the fumes reaching his nostrils. Still the baby sobbed. He turned and saw the mother clutching it, and Nico's expression was so severe the mother quailed.

'Sorry,' she said, trying to hush her child.

He shook his head, tried to tell the woman that he was not angry, but his throat was suddenly dry. He stared at the water and the island of Xanos ahead of him, felt the wind on his face and heard the screams of the baby. Despite the warm afternoon sun, a chill spread through Nico, and he felt a sweat break out on his face and for a moment thought he might vomit.

He stood, his legs for the first time unsteady, and he moved to the rail of the ferry and made himself walk away from the passengers. He was too proud to appear weak even in front of strangers, but still the baby's screams reached him.

Perhaps he was seasick, Nico told himself, dragging in air that did not soothe because it tasted of salt. But he could not be, for he sailed regularly. Weekends were often spent on his yacht—no, Nico knew this was something different.

Still the baby screamed and he looked towards Lathira, from where he had set off and then over to Xanos, where he was headed, and the foreboding did not leave him.

They docked and he walked briskly from the boat— decided he was not going to get used to public transport, that a helicopter would fly him back. Nico walked to a taxi and asked to be taken to the town church. He stared out of the window and did not respond to the driver's attempts at conversation, just stared out at streets that were somehow familiar. As they arrived at the church, he recognised it and could not fathom why, did not want to. Even climbing the steps, somehow he felt as if he were recalling a dream and Nico stood for a moment to steady himself before going in.

The bride was arriving and he watched as she stepped out of the car and a swarm of bridesmaids, like coloured butterflies, busily worked around her, brushing down her dress. The older one fiddled with the simple veil that would soon be lifted over the bride's face before entering the church. Nico realised, whether she was from the north or the south, Stavros had done incredibly well for himself for she was quite simply stunning. How wasted she would be on the groom.

Was it the dress? Nico mused as he watched her. It was simple and straight, yet it nipped in at the waist to show her voluptuous curves. Or perhaps it was the heavy, full breasts that were so absent on the rake-thin women he usually dated that were the allure. He was used to sculpted, exercised, false curves—yet this bride's body was lush. Her breasts moved as she lowered her head to thank her small flower girl, in a way the breasts he was used to holding never did—they were flesh, Nico knew, as was the curve of her bottom. There was a softness to her stomach that was natural. Her skin was creamy and pale for a local, and he could not take his eyes from her, felt the disquiet that had plagued him since he'd stepped onto the ferry subside as he quietly observed.

Her thick dark hair was worn up and how Nico would have liked to take it down. He could not make out the colour of her eyes from this distance but they glittered and smiled as she laughed at something that her brides-maid said—and it was her energy that was stunning, the smile and the laughter and the way she took her father's arm. Then he saw her still as the priest walked towards her, saw her tense for a brief moment and straighten her shoulders, saw the swallow in her throat and the smile slip from her face as everyone moved to their positions. It was more than nerves, Nico thought as she closed her eyes for a long few seconds. It was as if she was bracing herself to go in, but then her lovely face disappeared from view as the bridesmaid arranged the veil.

It was normal to be nervous, Connie told herself as the priest walked towards her, but suddenly it was real. The preparation for this day had been all-consuming, her father determined that his only child would have a wedding fit for this prominent family. He would show the people of Xanos and his friends in Lathira that, despite rumours to the contrary, he was doing well. For weeks, or rather months, Connie had been swept along on a tide of dress fittings, menu selections, dance lessons with Stavros, but only now as she stood behind her veil with the priest telling her it was time did it seem real.

This was her life: this was happening whether she wanted it or not.

No one knew of her private tears when her father had told her of the husband that had been chosen for her. And later, when she had confided in her mother that Stavros's words were cruel at times, her mother had told her to be quiet. Even when, awkward and embarrassed, she'd told her mother that he did not seem interested in her, that he had not so much as tried to kiss her, her mother had told her they had chosen a gentleman for her. That sort of thing was for when she was safely his.

A bride, Connie told herself as she sucked in air, was supposed to be nervous on her wedding day.

And a bride was supposed to be nervous about her wedding night.

Was she the last virgin bride?

The boys and, later, men of the island had been too nervous of her protective father to date her. How she'd yearned for fun and laughter…and, yes, romance, too.

But there had been none.

Even during her business studies in Athens, which she'd loved, she'd been guarded by her cousin; every move she'd made had been reported back to her family, till she had returned to the island and commenced work in her father's small firm.

As was expected.

'Kalí tíhi.' Her bridesmaid wished her luck and Connie closed her eyes as her father took her arm. He felt so frail Constantine wondered who was holding who up.

This was why she was here, Constantine reminded herself.

Her father's dearest wish, to see his daughter safely married.

It wasn't at all unusual on the island for the family to choose the partner. In fact, it was how things were done here. There was no question that she would disobey. Already she had put off this day for her studies. And she was…*fond* of Stavros, Connie told herself, even if his words were sometimes harsh. Love would grow, her mother had told her. They had chosen well for their daughter, she had been assured.

Yet there was a stab of grief as the priest commenced chanting, as the bridesmaid covered her face with the veil and the procession moved towards the church, grief for all she would now never know.

She was naive only in body. Of course she knew there were other ways for couples to meet—she had heard of them, read of them, gossiped about them with her more worldly friends during her studies. She had listened to their tales of flirting and fun, dates and romance, first kisses and reckless nights, break-ups and tears, and she wanted to sample each and every one of those things, but it was not to be.

And then she saw him and her heart stilled.

Like an omen.

Like a black crow on the steps he stood as if warning her not to go in.

Like the devil, dark eyes beckoned; and the sun was too hot on the top of her head. It was certainly her father holding her up now, because with one look at this man she was almost dizzy. Only one long look and it was as if she tasted for a second all that had been denied, all that would be denied if she climbed the steps.

He was surely the most beautiful man she had ever seen.

Tall, he lounged against a column, shamelessly staring, which, Connie told herself, people did to a bride.

But it was *how* he looked that had her stomach fold over itself. It was a different sort of look from any she had experienced.

His eyes roamed over her, and she felt her body burn.

Thank God for the veil, for beneath it she burnt red, her breathing tight in her chest; she could feel the prickly heat from her face spreading across her chest and down to her arms.

Brides blushed on their wedding day, Connie told herself as she slowly climbed the steps.

Except the burn in her body was not for the man who waited at the altar, or for guests whose heads would turn when she entered. Instead, the burning was for him. It was surreal, just bizarre, to be walking towards her future, and to see at that second a different route. And as his full mouth did not move into a smile, as his eyes compelled her, so strong was the pull, so fierce the attraction, so palpable the energy between them, she was sure, quite sure, that had she walked over to him, had she *run* to him as her body was telling her to, that his arms would be waiting; that now, right now, she could walk away, run away, and live a life that was hers.

'I can't.' Once past him she faltered at the door of the church, the smell of incense from the priest's burner making her feel sick. 'I can't do this.'

'It's nerves,' her father said kindly. 'Today—' her father's voice came from a distance '—is my proudest day…' Like waking from a dream, she was back in reality, and instead of looking backward to where his eyes still burnt on her bare shoulder, she looked forward, looked down the long aisle and saw her husband-to-be waiting.

Nico had seen her blush, had felt her start and wondered, too, what had just happened. It had felt, for a moment, as if they knew each other, as if their minds were speaking, the connection had been so strong, yet it had come from nowhere.

Perhaps they had once been lovers, Nico mused,

which would explain the blush that crept down her chest
and dappled her creamy arms.

He should remember, though, Nico thought, and not
out of guilt, for he had held so many women in his arms
that recall was often hard. Too many times an ex-lover
had galloped over to him then left in tears, because the
night she had treasured for so long didn't even merit a
fond memory for Nico. But as for this bride—her body,
that gorgeous round face and full ripe lips—surely he
would have remembered making love to a woman like
that.

He made his way into the church and chose to sit
quietly at the back rather than join his parents, for the
bride had reached her soon-to-be husband. He noted
the lack of response from Stavros: there was no smile
of appreciation; no eyes that looked in wonder. Nico
thought, *Had she been his...* And then he stopped that
thought process with a wry smile, for Nico did not believe in love, could not imagine spending his life with
only one other. His relationships were short-lived at
best, a night most times.

Her name was Constantine, he heard from the priest,
and it suited her, Nico thought.

He'd forgotten how long Greek weddings took—he
stood and sat on demand during the service of the be-
trothal and he toyed with just slipping away unnoticed
and heading for a bar before the crowning. The priest
blessed the rings and asked Constantine if she was willing. Nico saw the candle she was holding flickering her
shaking hands, and truly he wanted to walk over and

blow it out. He could feel her dangerous hesitation and willed her to listen to it.

For he knew she was more than this.

More than the stifling laws and traditions he had walked away from.

A place where appearance was everything, where there could be no debate, no expansion, no change.

Connie wondered, as she had wondered so many times, if there was more than this, heard the priest repeat the question, ask if she was willing, and again she wanted to run. Wanted to turn her head to the congregation, to see if those eyes would be waiting, and told herself she was being ridiculous.

This was the day she had been raised for; this was how her life was to be. Who was she to question her father, the traditions she had been born to? Finally she nodded, mumbled that she was willing, and almost heard the door close on all her secret dreams.

It did close, for on hearing that Nico moved from his pew and walked out of the church.

He went to a taverna that was waiting and ordered strong coffee and then thanked the bartender when he brought out an ouzo, too. Normally he did not drink it, it was too sickly and sweet for him, but the taste of anise on his lips and the burn as it hit his stomach had Nico order another. He stared out at a town that was somehow familiar—the dusty busy streets and colourful market, the bustle and chatter as a crowd of locals started to gather outside the church, waiting for the couple to appear. Nico pulled out his phone, was about to tell Charlotte to book him a suite on the south of the island—he would say hello to his parents and then get out—but it wasn't out of consideration to his PA that he put away his phone. Instead, he wanted to be here, Nico realised, wanted to sit in the café in the town square and soak in the afternoon sun. He liked the scent from the taverna and the variance in dialect here on Xanos that hummed in the background. As the newly wed couple appeared on the steps, Nico walked to the hotel and informed them of his arrival, saw the nervous swallow from the concierge, because certainly this man would expect the best.

'I will be joining the wedding,' Nico also informed him. 'Nico Eliades. I will sit with my parents.' He did not ask whether that could be arranged, neither did he apologise. Nico expected and always got a yes.

'Nico!' His mother seemed shocked to see him as he joined them at the table. 'Why are you here?'

'Some greeting,' Nico said. 'Normally you plead with me to attend these sort of functions.'

'Of course…' She gave a nervous smile, her eyes desperately searching the room for her husband who, seeing Nico, strode over immediately.

'This is a pleasant surprise.'

'Really?' Nico said, because his father's eyes said otherwise. 'You don't seem to pleased to see me.'

'It's not the sort of thing you are used to.' His mother said. 'The hotel is shabby…' His mother was an unbearable snob. It was a gorgeous old hotel and far from shabby. It had character and charm, two things, in his parents, that were lacking. 'Dimitri is mortified to hold the reception here. The sooner they get this girl back to Lathira where we can have a proper celebration, the happier we will all be. Really, Nico.' She gave him a saccharine smile. 'This place is not for you.'

'Well, I'm here now.' Nico shrugged, his words dripping with sarcasm when they came. 'What could be nicer than spending a day with my family?'

He ate, and sat bored through the speeches, deciding it had been foolish to come.

Women flirted.

Beautiful, gorgeous women. One in particular was to his usual taste and how easy it would be to take a bottle of champagne from a table, take her by the hand and go up to his room. Yet he glanced at Constantine as she danced with her husband, and silently felt regret, for she had spoilt his appetite for silicone tonight. All Nico could think was, Lucky Stavros.

It was the first time he had felt even a hint of envy toward Stavros.

The son of his father's business rival and competitive friend, always the children had been compared.

Always Nico had won.

Except on duty.

Nico had not gone into the family business—he had chosen to go alone. At eighteen, to the protests of his family, he had headed for the mainland, worked as a junior in banking and then, when still that had not satisfied, he'd headed to America. He had faked a better résumé, and how impressed they had been with the young Greek man who could read the stockmarket. How painstaking building his own portfolio had first been, but then, with passion and determination, he had scanned global markets, invested in properties when prices had crashed, sold them when the pendulum swung back.

It always did.

How easily Nico saw that. Could not understand how others could not, for they sweated and panicked and sometimes jumped, where Nico sat calm, watching and waiting for new growth in the fertile ashes.

Each visit back home he returned richer and, despite the fights in private, his father was proud that always his son was better.

It would, though, Nico decided, be hard to match the rare beauty of Stavros's bride.

Poor thing.

The thought jumped uninvited to the forefront of his mind as he watched her dance, not with her husband but to the tune of tradition. He watched her vie for her husband's attention, but he was too busy talking with his *koumbaros,* irritated when she tapped him on the shoulder and told him they must now dance. He watched as Stavros ran his hand down her bottom and then said something into her ear.

And then he saw her pull away.

A flash of hurt, anger perhaps, in her eyes and Nico knew it had not been a compliment that had come from Stavros's lips.

He was sure, because that was the way on Lathira,

as Constantine would soon find out, that even on her wedding night she had been criticised.

It was death by a thousand cuts, the world she had entered, and he had just witnessed the first.

She would be part of Lathira's social set—have lunch with the other trophy wives and then back to the gym the following morning to pay for it. They would seep the life from her till she was as polished and as hard as the rest, and Nico did not want to sit and witness even a moment of it. It had been a mistake to come. Nico did not do sentiment, did not enjoy weddings. All they did was cause a vague bewilderment—to share your life, your future, to entrust yourself to another?

He looked at the bride, who was not blushing but pale and visibly stressed, at his parents, who sat tense, at the couples that forced smiles and conversation, and he searched for something that might discount his theory that love did not exist. He looked around the room and there were two boys, raiding the table, laughing as they ordered cola from the waiters. Two brothers causing mischief, and he felt a twist in his soul that came from nowhere he could place.

'I'm going to retire.' He waited for the protest from his parents but the only protest he got was from the blonde whose name he couldn't for the life of him remember.

'Will we see you in the morning?'

'Perhaps.' Nico shrugged. 'Or I may leave early.'

'Come and see us on Lathira soon,' his mother said. 'It has been ages.'

'I'm here now,' Nico pointed out, because this visit had to count as one, for he would not be back for months now.

He wished he loved them.

As he walked out of the ballroom, Nico wished he was blind to their faults, but all he saw were greedy, ego-driven people.

He collected his room keys, was advised that his things were in his room, but instead of heading up there on a whim he turned and headed out to the streets.

Past the church and the taverna, along the road to the fishing boats and the fishermen who sat smoking and drinking on the beach. He followed a path that should not be familiar except he seemed to know where it led, and he walked, somehow at ease with the seamier side of town, past the late-night bars to the street that forked into cobbled alleys. He could hear breathing behind him and heavy footsteps but Nico felt no fear.

He saw the tired face of a hooker and the voice of a man behind him.

'How much?'

He saw her face shutter as she named her price and Nico felt his heart still.

He looked down the alley to where she would take the man and he heard the words repeat in his head.

How much?

He felt dread, for the first time he felt dread and broke the conversation.

'She's already booked.' He turned to the bloated,

greedy face and told him she was taken. All he did was shrug and move on.

'Since when?' The hooker sneered.

He did not want her, but he didn't want that man for her, either.

'Go home,' Nico said, and she swore at him in Greek, told him she was sick of do-gooders. Then her tirade stopped as he paid her plenty.

'What are you paying me for?'

'For peace,' Nico said, even if he did not understand his own response. He just wanted to stop the trade, to wipe out one injustice.

He walked the streets; he ran through the streets like a madman; the town clock chimed and he realised it was two a.m. He wanted away from this place and how it made him feel. He would be gone first thing in the morning, would go now to his room and order their best bottle of brandy, not the sickly ouzo that churned in his stomach still.

He walked briskly through the hotel foyer, bypassed the lift and took the stairs, two, three at a time, and when nothing could have halted him, something did.

A bride still in her dress, a half-drunk bottle in one hand, a crumpled heap on the stairs, crying.

'Leave me,' she sobbed, and he wanted to, did not want to sit on the stairs and ask her what was wrong, for he already knew.

Did not want to sit and tell her to hush, to dry her tears and to tell her to go back there, as his father would expect him to.

He did neither.

He took her by the hand and made her stand.

Felt her hot hand in his and he wanted all of her, wanted to hold her, to stop the tears, to comfort her.

'Leave me,' she begged. 'I'll be okay in a moment.'

She wouldn't be, Nico knew that. The champagne might dim her pain enough to send her back, but no doubt she'd need it again tomorrow, and another night and another…to get through the hell that would be her marriage, because Nico knew the truth.

'Come with me.' He took her by the hand and he led her.

'Come with me to my room.'

CHAPTER TWO

'HE'S GAY.'

He hadn't even got her through the door before she blurted it out, and Nico was surprised and rather proud that she did.

That she admitted what, after this night, she must never again say to another.

'Why,' was Nico's only response to the revelation as he turned the lights on in his room and saw it for the first time, 'have I been given the bridal suite?'

Tear-filled eyes looked around and she let out a slightly hysterical laugh—this, the room she had chosen when her father had booked the hotel, this, the room she had later envisaged being part of a magical night.

'Stavros changed the booking. He said that he wanted the two-bedroom suite. I thought it was so I could get ready away from him, instead he and his *koumbaros*...' She was wretched in her grief, the sobs getting louder, and he went to the bathroom and came out with a wad of tissues.

Nico could not help but give a wry smile as he looked

around. The maids must have assumed it was being used as the bridal suite and prepared the wrong room for the *happy* couple, for there were candles that had long since gone out, and petals on the bed, a bottle of champagne in an ice bucket. The ice had melted and was now water.

'When did you find out?' Nico asked, wincing on her behalf when she answered.

'Just before. When we got back to the room, when still he would not kiss me, when I begged…he told me…' Constantine sobbed. 'He even laughed that I hadn't worked it out, that I hadn't questioned why he never seemed to want me. I thought it was out of respect for this night.'

'You had no idea?' He had assumed she knew, that that was the reason for her hesitancy at the church. That she was going along with things, as so many others on the islands did.

'I thought things would be different after the wedding.' She still sobbed. 'That he was nervous of my father…men always are. I knew I didn't yet love him, but I thought it might grow, that we'd make it work.' She was so, so humiliated, so embarrassed. The kisses she had pressed on her new husband seemed to have repulsed him. She switched from shamed to furious. 'I'll take a lover,' she said defiantly, and Nico just stood there. 'I'll take ten!' And Nico suppressed a smile, but when the tears came again he saw the real depth of her grief, heard firsthand what was really distressing this beautiful bride.

'He knew.' She sobbed. 'My father knew. Why would he agree to that? He could have chosen better for me—he's a prominent man, he's the island's lawyer, surely I am worth more than this? I believed him when he said that this was the best choice for me, that other ways end in divorce. I trusted him to make the best choice for me. Why would he choose for his daughter a man who could never love me?'

Nico was quite sure he could hazard an accurate guess.

By local standards this had been a lavish wedding. Clearly her father was one of the island's wealthy—but how could a lawyer get rich when the people he served were poor? The celebrities in the south had their own legal teams, they would never choose the services of a local. Nico knew how things worked on Lathira, knew from his own family the lengths they would go to to get that next deal—it was why he wanted no part of it. He was sure it was no different here on Xanos. He could smell the corruption yet Constantine seemed to have no idea, and suddenly she was back to scared.

'I shouldn't have said anything about it to you.' Panic flared in her eyes as she realised who she was confiding in. "If Dimitri found out that your father knew about Stavros… Oh, God…' she whimpered. 'He's the one Dimitri always wants to impress…'

'Constantine. Your secret is safe.' His voice was clear and commanding, his words unwavering. So badly she wanted to believe in him, but surely she could not trust him. After all, he didn't even know her name.

'It's Connie,' she said. 'People I know call me Connie.'

'And if you knew me, then you would know that I do not speak with my father, other than about the food on the table or the temperature of the air. We do not speak of things.'

'You might now…'

'No,' Nico said. 'No.' He said it again, and it was up to her whether or not she believed him. 'I will say nothing,' Nico said. 'One day you might choose to, though.'

Her eyes jerked to his and she glimpsed that possibility.

Maybe when her father was gone, she could end this hell, but there was still her mother, her family, the reputation they lived and died by, and she simply could not do it to them, though Nico did not leave it there.

'I do know how hard it can be.'

She shot him a disbelieving look. She couldn't imagine anyone even attempting to put pressure on this strong, assertive man and getting away with it, but when he spoke next she realised that he just might understand.

'When I grew up, it was a given that I would go into the family business. That I would live in a house a few minutes away with my wife and children, that the family would sit together to eat at night and weekends. My first son would be named Vasos after my father.' She nibbled on her lower lip, his words painting her future, for even as Stavros had broken the news, he had told her that there would be children, that their first son would be named Dimitri. 'I broke away. I have made my own business. I come home now and then but always it is to a row. I have no interest in marriage, and—' his voice was definite '—I certainly never want children. It causes fights with my parents even to this day. I am their only son, their only child, and, as they tell me at every given chance, I am a bitter disappointment to them.'

She looked up at him and truly wondered how he could possibly disappoint. She had heard the envy in Dimitri's voice when he'd spoken of the Eliades and their rich and successful son, but from the way Nico was talking, the pressure from home was exactly the same for him. Yes, maybe he did understand all she was going through, maybe he did know how impossible it was for her.

'I'm an only child, too…' Connie said, her voice faltering because she had never really discussed such things, but he nodded with understanding and tentatively she carried on. 'So much is expected from me. So much of their happiness hinges on me.'

'When you are in it,' Nico explained, 'you cannot judge it, you just know that something is wrong. When you break away…' She closed her eyes because there was no chance of that, but Nico spoke on. 'When you clearly see all you have to sacrifice to make them happy, maybe you will choose to be happy for yourself.'

'Some sacrifice.' She tried to be brave, to look at the bright side. 'I will be living in Lathira, in a beautiful home, entertaining…'

'The perfect wife,' Nico interrupted. 'You will lunch

with your friends, dressed in your secret… A woman, a wife, perhaps even a mother… ' And she started to cry a little, because he was right, it had all been worked out.

'Stavros said that we will have children, that there are ways for me to get pregnant without…' She choked rather than say 'without touching me' but Nico heard every unspoken word and could happily have crossed the corridor and thumped Stavros and then her father, too, for all they would so readily deny her. Of course there were ways for her to have children, to play perfect—he could see her future, could picture it, because so many people here lived mired in their secrets. He looked into her eyes and found out that they were, in fact, the darkest of blue and surely she deserved better. He wanted her to see she could have so much more than the life she was being forced into.

'When you join your new friends at the gym, when you shop with them and you try on a dress and they tell you that you look beautiful, that if you buy that dress then Stavros will not be able to keep his hands off you…' He saw tears fill her eyes again and perhaps he should stop, but this would be her truth. 'Will you be able to admit to these so called friends that not once has he touched you?'

'Please stop.'

'Tonight you danced… What did he say that upset you?'

She didn't answer and Nico walked over, and she wrapped her arms around her body as if to cover it.

'What did he say?' Nico quietly demanded, and she moved her hands down to her hips.

'That this…' she clutched her figure '…could be improved.'

'Tell him he is never to speak to you that way and mean it,' Nico said, but as he looked at her he changed his mind, for surely she should not stay. 'Tell him that you won't live like this.'

'I cannot.'

'You could get an annulment.' She screwed her face up at the impossibility, just too embedded in the ways of the island to take such a step. It wasn't his job to save her, it wasn't his place to insist she be strong, for after all he would be gone from Xanos in the morning.

'Then you do your best to survive your life.' Nico gave a half-smile as he left her to it—it was not for him to persuade her otherwise. 'Take your lover.' He gave a shrug. 'Take ten.'

'I can't…' She closed her eyes in dread. 'What if he were not discreet, what if people found out…?'

'You care too much what others think.'

And then she cried, different tears now, not angry, or bitter, but she cried for all that would be denied to her, for a loveless, sexless future and all the hope she had pinned on this night. Her grief so deep, her pain so real it could not help but move him. He went over to the chair and wrapped her in his arms. He thought he would comfort her; he was unsure of his motives, but the feel of arms around her, the scent of him close and all she had suffered tonight had her mouth move to his. He felt her clumsy, desperate kiss on his lips and closed his eyes, not in passion but restraint.

He moved his mouth away, pulled his head back and heard her sob. He realised he had added to her humiliation as he did to her what Stavros must have done, so very many times.

He looked down at her hands, which were shaking in her lap.

'Where is your ring?'

'I threw it at him,' she said. 'I'm never putting it back on.' And then he saw a tear slide out of her eye at the hopelessness of it all, for tomorrow, he was quite sure, it would be on. She would do her duty, to everyone but herself.

'I'll go back.' She went to stand but her legs woud not obey and for a moment she sat. 'Thank you.' She gave a very wan smile. 'Thank you for talking to me, thank you for your kind words, and I apologise for suggesting you might gossip…'

'I am discreet.'

'Thank you.' She took a deep breath, as one would when preparing to dive into cold water. 'I'd better go back.'

'I meant…' He should just let her go, it was no business of his, but the thought of her going back to lie in a bed alone, of Constantine crying herself to sleep, of all her wants unfulfilled, moved Nico when usually sob stories did not. 'You said you were worried a lover may not be…'

Hope flared inside her and he must have seen it,

because instantly he quashed it. 'I will not be your long-time lover, I am no one's escape…' He saw her eyes shutter. 'But I will be with you tonight.'

'Just tonight?' She wanted more than that: she wanted weekends in Athens and discreet meetings in hotels and phone calls and all the passion that had been denied. She wanted so much more than one night with him.

'Only tonight.' He looked at her, his eyes roamed the body he had been thinking about for hours now, the virgin bride, who would stay that way if not for him. 'You come to my bed, I will show you what your husband denies you—all you miss out on if you choose to live this lie…'

'I have no choice.'

'Always we have choices,' Nico said, and this was his—to choose not to examine his feelings tonight. His mind was black and here was light. The streets of Xanos had unsettled him, stirred emotions that he sorely wanted gone. He wanted diversion and here it had been delivered to him in the shape of a tear-streaked, beautiful virgin.

He stood and she took his hand and did the same. She stared at the room and it was the wedding night of her dreams—just the wrong man. Then she looked again, because if she was completely honest, dangerously, guiltily honest, Stavros would never have fulfilled that fantasy. Here now before her *was* the man of dreams, and he could be hers—but only for one night.

CHAPTER THREE

LOVE, like marriage, for Nico would never happen.

As she excused herself for a moment, Nico stood and looked out to the window, to the inky ocean and a sky devoid of stars or moon, and he knew he had been right in the decision he had made long ago.

Nico did not believe in love.

He had nothing to base that on—his parents' marriage had been long and seemingly happy, his aunts uncles and cousins on the mainland were all wed. It had been assumed by his family that Nico would have long ago carried on the family name, yet the idea was alien to him.

In love you lost.

Where that belief came from he did not know, but it was as real and as ingrained as was the fact he rose with the dawn each morning. And Nico lost at nothing—so he chose not to love.

To give your heart, to commit, was unfathomable to Nico.

The only reason, as far as he could see, for marriage

was to have children and Nico certainly did not want that. For to love and to lose, where a child was concerned, nothing could be more horrific and surely it was never worth the pain.

So his heart remained closed.

He turned and saw her as she nervously walked into the room, as close to a bride of his own as he would ever get.

And were it somehow possible, were his heart to have chosen one for him, had he dared to even consider it, then surely she would be the one.

He saw her cheeks grow pink under his scrutiny, his eyes taking in the luscious curves, the untouched terrain of her body that for tonight was his to roam. He could feel her nerves, her excitement, the tension in the room that was all a wedding night should be—and surely now he could give in and hold her.

His head was full from the streets, images at the forefront that he wanted shadowed, and her mouth would be a sweet distraction. He crossed the room towards her, traced her naked arms, felt the rise of goose bumps beneath his fingers; and she was not just nervous, he realised, she was literally shaking with fear.

'Maybe this is not what you want...'

She heard him about to retract, realised he had mistaken her nerves, but it wasn't just nerves or inexperience that had her shaking, it was the overwhelming feeling of him close. It was the man who was holding her now, because he made her weak and he had not even kissed her. Feelings never encountered were rushing in, and as his mouth lowered to hers, as his full lips met hers, so clumsily she responded, rued her inexperience under such a skilled mouth. His moved so slowly and hers did not know how...and the taste of his tongue as it parted her lips was so sharp and cool, so intimate to feel, that her head moved back in startled surprise.

'I haven't...' She screwed her eyes closed, embarrassed at her lack of skill, because no *almost* a virgin was she. 'I've never been kissed.'

He looked down at her mouth, at lips that seemed made solely for that and could not believe they were his alone. 'You haven't kissed?'

'Never. I have done nothing.' She sobbed it out, for there had been no kissing, no touching, no petting, and she was angry for her own naivety, as if some honour had kept Stavros from so much as touching her. And there was shame for her spurned kisses, too, for, though she had tried to push it aside, though she had tried to tell herself otherwise, she had felt rejection over and over from her fiancé. She had clumsily flirted to no avail, had pressed lips and told herself as he had jerked his head back that her touch did not repulse, yet somewhere deep inside she had known that it had. 'I thought tonight, I hoped tonight things would finally be different...'

'And it shall be,' Nico said, and he vowed, he would take care of her, would catch her up with her own body and take her from the age of eighteen to twenty-four in the hours allowed them tonight. He would show her all her body could be and leave her a woman by morning.

'We will take things slowly,' he promised. 'I will show you each and every thing you have been missing. Now, for a first kiss…' He tried to think himself younger, tried to picture a long-ago night that had never happened, 'Perhaps we are walking back from the taverna at the market square…'

She smiled as she pictured that thought. 'My house is just around the corner from there.'

'Then I am walking you home…' He could, he actually could picture it. 'And I stop you.' He took her wrist. 'And I turn you to face me.'

He lowered his head and she was breathless in anticipation and then she felt his lips on hers, but more gently this time, a mouth that moved only slowly, a mouth that gave her time to warm, to feel, to accept the press and the gift of soft flesh from another. This mouth did not tighten or jerk away when she pushed a little harder still, and it was sweet but it was wanton, for how could it be not when she was drenched by the manly scent of him?

'And then…' Nico said, and she breathed as she moved from her first kiss, 'when all night you have been wanting, when you have been out for dinner, when you have walked on the beach, but still you are wary, still you know not the motives of the other, when all you want is a taste of the promise to come.' This, Nico decided, was the kiss he would give her were he young and first dating, were they sandy from walking on the beach. It was all new for him, too—for he had been swept into manhood on a surge of testosterone, had learnt at the altar of older woman, the cruise boats bringing them hungry and desperate for a few hours' escape from their neglected lives. Loaded with sambuca and a night dancing on tables, they had climbed down to his outstretched hand and then fallen to him. Their kisses had been desperate and frantic, the sex hot and urgent, and it had left him replete for a while, but, like the tide as it turned, he had been left hollow after—till the next time and then the next.

Had she been there then, Nico decided, had it been her in his youth, he would have kissed her like this. Still softly he kissed her, his hands moving down her arm and to her waist. He held her from his centre as his tongue, slowly this time, slipped in, and this time she accepted it, this time she explored the smooth, moist flesh and relished the taste of him. He fought now to hold her from him, for he wanted to pull her hips into him. But not yet, he told himself, for right now it could be different. They would have all night for this, all night to kiss, because there, in the world they had now created, there would be the promise of more tomorrow.

His tongue was delicious, but it made her greedy for more, she now wanted the press of his mouth as it had once been, she wanted more urgency and her mouth demanded more. Her hands, in reflex, moved from loose limbed by her side up to his shoulders, up past his neck and into his hair. She sucked on the taste of him, and he took her away, to a date they had never had, but seemed now to exist, to hot peppered calamari bought at the taverna and eaten on the beach. So real was her dream she could hear the ocean as he kissed her, her feet surely not in stilettos but resting on sand. After a moment he halted her, his breathing a touch ragged, his words husky when finally they came.

'Now I have to take you home.'

'I don't want to go.' She did not, not back to her father. She wanted her next date, wanted to find out what Nico would do, how she might tempt him.

'Now,' Nico said, 'I've taken you for dinner...twice,' he added, and gave her a smile, a smile he had never given another, an intimate smile, not for the game they were playing, more for the dream they were sharing. He looked at his bride, who was not his but felt it, then at a dress more complicated than even this skilled lover had encountered. His fingers plucked the row of tiny buttons that ran in a line down her spine and she wanted to tell him they were for show only, but the feel of his fingers, probing, exploring, had her mouth close in pleasure as his lips lowered to her neck and he kissed the sensitive flesh there.

He loved this.

More than ever before, he loved the slow exploration of a woman, her pliant and wanting in his arms as his fingers probed the thick satin, as his other hand cupped her waist and then explored it, and, oh, the triumph of locating a concealed zip.

'You would stop me,' Nico said, as there just beneath the hollow of her armpit he found the hidden prize and started to slowly pull down the zipper. 'You would stop me, or wriggle, or warn me…' he said, as slowly he slid it down.

'Why would I stop you?' Constantine said as his mouth kissed her neck deeper, as she felt the breeze of air on her torso, then the warmth of his hand slipping in. 'Why would I stop you when it feels so sublime?'

And words should not have such an effect, but so blatantly pleasurable was her response he had to hold her back, for to press her into him now would end the dream in a matter of moments. He wanted her on the bed, he wanted so badly to be inside her, and yet he made himself wait. It was a long, hard wait that was threatened for a moment as he made light work of her strapless bra and a breast dropped heavy into his palm.

His warm hands caressed her, and indescribable was the pleasure—hands that were not hers on her body, moving in ways she would never have thought of, and then when she thought it could not be any better, when his thumb pressed into her aching nipple, when he stroked it till it felt as if he was stroking right inside her, when surely it could not be more pleasurable, the lips on her neck slid down. The lips that were the first ever to kiss her moved wet and warm to a nipple that hurt in anticipation, and the blow of air from his mouth should have cooled, but it produced a heat from a place where heat had never existed and he kissed her breast as expertly, as hungrily and deliciously as he had kissed her mouth. Her fingers pressed and knotted into his hair and she worried how she might stay standing, how she had lived a life without knowing the pleasure of this, how nearly she *had* lived a life where this pleasure was denied her. He moved away from her breast to her face, and she wanted him back there instead of the cool air on her wet skin.

Then she didn't want, because she got.

She got what Nico had wanted but had withheld for longer than he could have imagined. With one definite move, looking at her, awaiting her response, he drew her to where she belonged, against him. He pulled her deftly in and he met the giddy height of relief from wanting, because now his aching groin had the support of her warm body; but it did not satisfy, not even for a second, for instantly it demanded more.

He saw her eyes widen as she felt the solid length of his arousal, saw her lips close and a nervous, excited swallow as he pressed in harder again.

And again, till she was pressing now into him.

And they both tasted for the first time *real* teenage kisses, willing the other on to a sweet forbidden place. He shrugged off his jacket and it was Connie who dealt with his tie and then somehow they were moving to the bed. Nico kicked off his shoes; Connie frantically tore at his shirt buttons till he lay there beside her, his bare feet sliding between her stockinged calves, her naked breasts against his exposed chest. To have skin on skin deepened their kiss, till he suckled on her tongue in a decadent disclosure of what he intended next.

His hand roamed over the curve of her bottom, scooped her hungry body right into his and she wanted her dress fully off, but he would not let her miss this lesson, would not, though he was tempted, deny her what long ago should have been hers.

How could he not want her?

As his fingers slid up beneath her dress, his question was not aimed at Stavros but at the fools who had feared her father, for had he been there, had he lived on this island, had they met before, then this moment would have been his a very long time ago.

She could feel his fingers, inching up the fabric and then sliding between the tender flesh of her inner thigh, and in reflex rather than refusal she clamped her legs together, could not fathom he wanted to touch her there.

'Just,' Nico breathed, and kissed as, despite her flesh's protest, still he moved higher, 'as a good girl would do.'

'I don't want to be good,' Connie said, as contrarily her legs tightened, yet her mind willed his hand higher.

'Then relax,' Nico said, as the vice of her thighs tightened around his hand.

'I don't know how to.'

'But you want me to carry on?' Nico checked, though he was sure, quite sure of her answer.

'Oh, yes.'

'Then all you have to do is trust me.'

Absolutely she did.

'Where are we?' she whispered. 'Where have you taken me?'

'For a drive,' Nico whispered, 'and soon you have to be home. We've stopped on the hill…and now,' Nico said, 'before I take you home I'm going to take you to heaven.' And she was there in his car, and much younger, and so, too, was Nico. She forced herself to breathe, to not think just for a second of what he was doing, to rest her mouth on his neck and just breathe in his scent. When she parted her legs the necessary fraction, his hand crept higher and she braced herself, for what she did not know; but he was more patient than she dared hope, his hand rested on her panties. He kissed her as she accustomed herself to the weight and the warmth and then as he kissed her hair, her cheek, her closed eyes, her head was too heavy and it sank in the pillow, his hand slid into her panties and expertly explored her.

She was so tender that surely soon she would tell him to stop, especially as probing fingers stretched her, and then she went to halt him again as his thumb pressed harder, but there were tiny, almost imperceptible beats of pleasure as his hand worked on. Tiny pulses that mirrored a rhythm that was rising inside, and she tried to stop, to wriggle away, but her body refused to move from this masterstroke. So she stayed, and she found just how much she had been missing. She came to his hand and did not want ever to go back and then Nico stopped, kissed her breathless, and told the shell of her ear what would be next. How it could have happened in the different world they had created, one where youth was shared at the same time, one where he was nicer, kinder, more trusting, one where he cared intensely for the woman in his arms. He told her how then he might have progressed.

'The next time we dated…' he whispered, 'I would want more from you. All week it would have been driving me crazy, trying to picture…'

He knelt up on the bed and pulled the dress down past her waist and removed it, and she made a small token gesture of modesty, gripped the fabric and then loosened it, because his gaze made her warm and utterly devoid of shame. All that was left was shoes and panties, and he dealt with the former, kissed her toes and then her soles till her feet curled around his hungry mouth. He found a sliver of flesh that was surely linked by a thread to where his fingers had just been because her hips rose from the pillow and he slid in between her calves. Nico had to pause and breathe a moment as he gazed at the pleasure that beckoned and the treasure that lay beneath the satin panties that were soaked from his earlier caress. He would wet her more with his mouth, Nico decided, would have her ripe and moist so as not to hurt her, except his virgin bride had different ideas.

'I would have, too.' Constantine said, and she saw him frown just a little as he tried to piece together a conversation when his mind was certainly elsewhere. 'I would have been thinking about you, too—wanting to see you.' Her hands moved up and slid down his open shirt, and she saw the shoulders she had leant on, the arms that had held her, the rise and fall of his chest and the lick of his lips as still he looked where no one had, as her body beckoned his mouth there, so badly she did want to see him. 'Let me see you.'

Nico stood and undressed and Constantine watched—excited, curious and, when she saw him, filled with trepidation, but her mind quietened that, for he was too beautiful to fear.

'And then?' Constantine asked, because she wanted what came next.

'And then...' Nico said, as he knelt back on the bed between her thighs and looked down at her waiting body, and for a moment tried to think of what next to tell her, what the next instalment of their story might be. Then he found it, and no imagination was required, for it was all right here.

'He waited,' Nico said. 'Till the night he took his bride to bed.' He paused for a moment, felt as if he *had* dated her, had lived his life here, that this moment, the future, truly was theirs. He looked down at her nervous, brave, but somehow trusting, and he felt like he would have had—had he loved her.

His hands slid down her panties and she moved her hand to hide herself, but there beneath such a tender gaze there was nothing Connie wanted to hide from.

He turned, annoyed with himself, for his jacket was on the floor, but she halted him as he went to climb from the bed.

'I went on the Pill for my wedding.'

Foolish girl to say that. Later he would warn her to trust no one with that knowledge but him. But he did not want to think of others and later he wanted to stay in a place where this was their night.

And selfishly, too, he wanted.

Wanted her in a way he had never before, a way that made him disregard his own strict rules, but only for her.

'Will it hurt?' Connie asked, but did not require an answer, because she knew there and then that whatever the pain it would not compare to the pain of tomorrow when Nico was gone.

'A little, perhaps.' His mouth was on her ear and then on her mouth and he kissed her in a way that she wanted, a fierce, deep kiss, his arms wrapped around her. She could feel the roughness of his thighs between hers; but his kiss was so urgent it claimed most of her attention. It was a kiss she had to race to keep up with, a kiss that bruised her mouth and scratched at her face, and she would not have had it any other way for even a moment.

His kiss was so hard it took away her breath and demanded her mind, so much so she could not fear those first explorative probes, and then his kiss stopped and she felt a sear of pain as he entered and, even stretched by his fingers, still it hurt more that she had thought it would. Her breath clamped in her throat as she bit down a sob, and then he moved when she prayed that he wouldn't and then he moved back and then in deeper again, and then it hurt, but not as much, and then his mouth was there at her ear and then she wasn't hurting. His words soothed, his endearments real, said as if he were her husband, and then when he moved faster within, Connie moved, too, forgot forever that once she'd been hurting and rose and wrapped around him.

She welcomed him in deeper. The last rapid thrusts from Nico, a signal her body heeded, and with him she went to a place that would live forever in her heart. The sound of his release met her scream and she wanted to stay there, with Nico, in the place they had created. But the pulse of her body slowed and slowly she remembered to breathe again, and a little later, when surely she should go back to her room, surely it would be dangerous to fall asleep, she let her body rest when he rolled into her. She would sleep a while in his arms and be with Nico on her wedding night.

He could hear the clock chime five times and for once fought the instinct to instantly awaken. He wanted to pull her warm body towards him, to make slow predawn love, not face the morning and the thoughts that last night had plagued him.

Nico reached for her body and then fought to resist: there was something too intimate about making love in the morning. In the long run he had found it better to leave things at last night, and this morning he chose to uphold his finding, because if had her again, he might then persuade her, might encourage her to stand up to her family, at what cost to her, though?

He looked over to where she slept deeply beside him.

How could he tear her from everything she knew, even if she didn't like it, with promises he knew he could not keep?

So instead when he moved it was to wake her.

'You should go back.'

It was a cruel awakening.

She wanted to stay in her dream, her wedding night, with this gorgeous man beside her. She did not want to go back, but she knew that she had to so she climbed out of the bed, pulled on her clothes and the dress he had so lovingly taken off. She wanted him to halt her.

Wanted him to tell her that she didn't need to go back, but she knew that it wasn't his place to, that she could only make that decision by herself.

'Thank you.' It was a strange way to end such a passionate night, but when Connie thought how it could have been, how wretched she had felt on the stairs last night, how without him she might never have known such bliss, her words were indeed heartfelt.

'Constantine...' As she walked out of the door he called out and she froze for a moment, the silence in the air shifting, because if she turned around she would be back in his bed and somehow they both knew it.

It was not for him to save her.

'It's Connie.' She opened the door and forced herself to walk out, to walk the agonising steps to her suite. In her bedroom she showered and put on the beautiful lace nightdress she had chosen for her wedding night, and climbed into the cold empty bed.

This would be her life if she stayed with the lie for even a day, Connie knew it. She was more grateful than Nico could ever know for their night. It had been so much more than sex—it had shown her how life should be.

Could be, Connie thought with a shiver of fear, but that would mean hurting so many people.

CHAPTER FOUR

HE WOKE before he jumped.

Had trained himself to open his eyes as soon as the lurch in his chest appeared, rather than have the beauty in his bed feel the jerk of his body beside her.

It was that or sleep every night alone, and Nico had no intention of doing that.

He hadn't had the dream in ages, but when Constantine had left and he had drifted back to sleep he had almost anticipated it—for yesterday something had stirred within him. The walk last night through the streets of Xanos had felt like a return to his familiar dream.

Where he lay paralysed, yet watching himself walk, talk, breathe, live.

A dream where his arms and legs were motionless, yet there he was walking around.

He hated the dream, hated lying there motionless, unable to move, unable to communicate with the version of himself he was watching.

Nico rolled over and her scent was there in bed beside

him—and there was regret for not making love to her this morning, for not breaking his steadfast rule. For once he was tempted to close his eyes, to give into his body and slip back to his thoughts, but he had trained himself too well and instead got out of bed and showered and dressed. He didn't shave and neither did he dress carefully, just pulled on the trousers he had worn last night and topped them with a black fitted shirt.

He toyed, only momentarily, with joining his family for breakfast, but not exactly relishing the prospect he decided otherwise. Given London was two hours behind them, he was for once kind to the long-suffering Charlotte, who arranged all his travel and other things, and he rang down himself to ask the concierge to arrange transport to take him back to the mainland. He didn't want to go to Lathira and he certainly wasn't going back on that ferry.

'To where?' the concierge asked, 'and will you need a connection?' for he could arrange a helicopter or seaplane to Volos and then a flight to Athens. For a beat of a moment Nico wished he'd rung Charlotte, for he didn't actually know where he was going. Always his time was accounted for and he did not like the feeling this unexpected day off gave him. He had properties everywhere but they were all investments. His job was so global he preferred hotels. His yacht was moored in Puerto Banus in Spain, which was perhaps becoming his base, for Nico was half considering buying a property there, not as an investment, though, but as a home.

'Just get me to Athens,' Nico said and rang off. He

would decide later, because, after yesterday's episode, a day on the ocean did not particularly appeal.

It never entered his head he would see her that morning—surely the facade should mean the happy couple breakfasted in bed, but as the lift doors slid open there she was with Stavros. She looked stunning and groomed, every bit a Lathira wife—her make-up immaculate, no trace of last night's crying evident, the elevator fresh with expensive fragrance, when Nico would have preferred the scent of her sex.

'*Kalimera.*' Nico greeted them and for the first time in his entire life he felt heat in his neck, in his ears and, as the liftman pressed the button, Nico found out how it felt to blush.

Not that Connie saw it.

Her own face was surely purple, her eyes staring down at her brand-new shoes. Stavros, unaware of the new charge in the air, stood beside her—but there was absolutely no guilt on her part. Her so-called husband had, after all, been with a lover of his own on their wedding night. Instead the burn in her cheeks was solely down to Nico, her body flaming in instinctive response, her cheeks firing at the memory of his mouth, his hands and all he had, last night, taught her to be.

'*Kalimera,*' Stavros said and nudged her, the dutiful wife, who must, he had told her, always perform, always look the part, entertain... And she opened her mouth to extend the greeting, to speak as she should, to act as she should, to greet her lover as a guest, and in her first act of defiance this morning she decided she would not. Connie stood instead, eyes forward, and slowly she blinked. She did not want to open her eyes to how things would be if she played along with the charade. She felt the nudge in her ribs again from Stavros, an irritated prompt which again she ignored.

And Nico knew it.

Though he stood in front of them, Nico was acutely aware of what was going on, could hear Stavros's angry breathing, could see, in the highly polished doors, him turn to his newly belligerent wife. There was an unseen hint of a smile on Nico's lips as behind him the sleeping dragon within her awoke.

But as they stepped out of the lift he stood for just a brief moment and watched as Stavros took his wife's hand and they headed to the restaurant. Now he was not smiling, for she was still, Nico noted, minus her wedding ring, the row in the bedroom spilling outwards, and he was worried for her. Not, Nico told himself, because of closeness they had shared, worried as you would be for anyone. For he had stood up to his family, had turned away from the family business, from the island, had refused the direction to take a suitable wife and deliver the promise of rapid grandchildren—and even for a man as mentally tough as Nico, it had been hard. How much harder for Constantine, for a married woman, for the golden only child of her parents, to turn the mighty tide now?

'Sir…' The concierge interrupted his thoughts, abject in his apology, especially for such an esteemed guest, but the hotel was already struggling to accommodate the demands of the wedding guests, and to have Nico Eliades added to the list had spun behind the scenes into chaos. No matter how he had juggled, the poor man had to now tell his esteemed guest that his transport would be another fifteen minutes.

At best.

'Perhaps you would like breakfast while you wait.'

Nico was about to decline for he never ate breakfast. He operated better hungry, black coffee his only charge till lunchtime, but, yes, he might as well say farewell to his parents.

Not that they seemed particularly pleased to see him. His mother almost jumped out of her skin when he approached the table.

'Nico!' Her exclamation was horrified, then rapidly changed to pleasant surprise. 'I thought you'd left.'

'Clearly not,' Nico said.

'When?' His father did not even an attempt to greet him, just demanded to know when he would be gone— and Nico had not, from the day he had turned eighteen, given in to his father's demands, and he didn't start now.

'I'm not sure. Perhaps I will do some sightseeing.' He had no intention, of course, he was just testing their reaction.

'You, sightseeing?' His mother smiled brightly, but it was so blatantly false that Nico was quite sure he could have leant over and peeled it from her well made-up face. 'The only views you like are from your yacht or five-star hotel windows.'

'I would like to see more of the island,' Nico said.

'I'm surprised we never came before—I always thought it was a miserable place…' Because that was how his parents had described it, Nico realised, over and over. Whenever Xanos had been mentioned, they had turned up their noses, told him it wasn't worth the time… 'It's really quite charming, I'd like to see it for myself.' His eyes halted whatever was about to come from his mother's mouth, even his father stayed quiet. 'Is there a problem?' Nico never dodged issues.

'Of course not,' his mother said, far too quickly.

There was no silver service, his mother was quick to point out, but coffee was quickly brought over to him and Nico took a sip and watched as Constantine stood chatting to some guests as Stavros made his way over and duly took her hand.

It was not jealousy that assailed him as he watched another man take her hand, it was something far deeper, something that incensed, and perhaps it incensed her, too, for she walked off from her husband. Nico saw her rather pointed drop of his hand as she went over to the breakfast buffet, and that knot of nervousness for her was back in his stomach.

You don't mess with these people.

There were rules and there were ways, hundreds upon thousand of unspoken things that were expected, that were done without question, and there was a tinge of regret for telling Constantine she had choices, when in reality she had none.

'I'm going to get some breakfast.' He would break his rule for her—and not just about eating. He went into his pocket and pulled out his business card, not the one he gave his lovers. Nico had two phone numbers, one for women that rang frequently but was answered rarely and changed all too often, the other number his permanent one.

'*Kalimera,*' Nico said for the second time that morning as he joined her at the breakfast buffet.

'*Kalimera.*' She answered for herself, she certainly did not need Stavros's prompting.

'How are you?' His voice was low and soft and the concern in it almost made her break down.

'Trying to choose…' And though her eyes wandered over the fruit, they were speaking not about fruit but in their own coded language.

'Be careful.' His hand was completely steady as he spooned some yoghurt into a bowl, but, as choices went, Connie made the wrong one, blueberries not the best fruit when one's hand was shaking so.

'Look, Constantine, if you need anything…'

'It's Connie,' she muttered, because it was who she was, a girl from a village, the golden child of a family that had made good. And if she did what her heart told her to, then she would surely destroy them.

'Not to me,' Nico said, and then he placed the business card on the bench. When he'd safely gone, she collected it, the weight of paper heavy in her hand, but her heart lighter for it. Just a small slip of card, but it was, Connie knew, her most valued possession.

'Eat later.' Stavros was beside her. 'We need to socialise.'

She turned to her husband. 'We need to talk.' But he wasn't about to listen to her, so she did as she was told, but only for now, and as she turned she saw the concierge approach Nico. She had to stand and make small talk, while out of the corner of her eye she was watching him, how effortlessly elegant he looked. The restaurant blazed with Lathira's and Xanos's Sunday and wedding best. It reeked of perfume and was filled with clean-shaven or well made-up faces, gold on fingers and necks and ears. And there Nico stood, unshaven, almost, her heart shivered, unkempt, for his shirt was a bit crumpled and his trousers were the same ones he'd had on the day before. But he stood out, not for that reason. He stood out for he commanded attention in a way that new clothes and heavy Greek gold never could.

She watched as he left, as all the good in her life walked out of the room without a backward glance, and, as she had yesterday, she wanted to run to him.

To run with him.

To be free.

CHAPTER FIVE

'I'VE changed my mind.'

The concierge was excellent, Nico decided, because apart from the bulge of veins in his neck, Nico would not have known the inconvenience he was causing. 'I would like to stay for another night here in Xanos. For now, I would like a driver to be arranged, one who can take me around the island. I do not know for how long.'

It was no trouble, the concierge assured him, no trouble at all.

'And…' He turned and gave an unusual request, one he would not have given had he stopped to think about it. 'My room is not to be disturbed.'

'I will have the maids just deliver fresh towels and make up the bed.'

'It is to be left,' Nico said, and for the second time in a lifetime, he almost blushed.

And Nico tried not to notice a middle-aged couple being shepherded, protesting, out of a vehicle, their luggage unloaded. In just a few moments the concierge led him out to his driver, who was a local. His name was George, he informed Nico as he climbed in.

'Anything you want to know, just ask.' George turned and looked over his shoulder as the car slid off. 'Have I driven you before?'

'I've never been to Xanos,' Nico said. 'Perhaps in Lathira, or on the mainland.'

'I've never been off the island.' George shrugged. 'You look familiar. Are you sure…?'

'You're mistaken,' Nico said, because he did not like small talk, or pointless chatter, but 'familiar' was a word that would repeat in his soul throughout the day. George took him down streets and through the town, along the curved mountains, to viewpoints that looked out to the ocean, and Nico felt something he hadn't even known was missing. He felt peace in the midst of confusion, a peace he had never known.

'I want to see the south.'

That caused a flurry of grumbles from George. 'It's all changed now,' he moaned. 'You have to pay to go there. There's only one road and there's a toll—there's even a watchman. They say it's to keep the press away, but it's as much to keep us locals out. He might not let us through…'

'He'll let me,' Nico said, because it was never otherwise, and sure enough, as the tollman peered into the back of the car and saw Nico lounging there, they were waved on immediately.

'It was always the poor side,' George explained, and for once Nico wanted to hear from his driver and asked him questions, encouraged him to speak on. 'The soil is more fertile in the north, that is where vines and orchards are, and the markets and ferry, too—really the south was just for local fishing, but not now.'

As the car swept along the beach road, even Nico, who was used to luxury, was taken aback by the contrast to the north of the island. Huge homes were carved into the rocky hillside. Yachts were out for their Sunday sail, but it had none of the charm of Puerto Banus; there was a certain sterility to the place and Nico was less than impressed.

'It would be good for the island's economy, though?' Nico asked, because that the was the sort of talk he was interested in, but George shook his head. 'They come here for seclusion, they don't eat in our restaurants and the developer uses his own men for the building. Really, it has done nothing for us…'

Nico could see what he meant as they drove: the houses were stunning, vast properties that overlooked the ocean, but the main street was nothing like the bustling town of Xanos, the aroma-filled town centre on the north of the island where yesterday he had sat. Here it was a sanitized version, with an exclusive hotel and smart designer boutiques, trendy cafés and restaurants.

'Which serve what foreigners think is Greek,' George explained, and Nico found himself smiling as they drove on. 'These aren't done yet,' George said. 'This was how it once looked.' And this was the real Xanos, Nico decided and told George to slow down. Simple houses were dotted in the hillside, but the once-loved gardens were now overgrown and neglected, the bull-dozers idle for the weekend but waiting to move in soon. There was a small taverna they drove past, where tradesmen now ate and drank, George explained, and what was left of the locals, but soon they, too, would be gone.

'They're all sold,' George said as Nico moved for his phone. 'He bought up the lot—there are a few locals that lease from him, but only till the work is complete and he's done with them.'

'Who?' Nico asked, but George didn't know.

'Some rich Australian.' Lack of information didn't stop Nico. Neither did the fact that it was Sunday. Even if it was her one weekend off, he rang an eternally patient Charlotte and told her to make enquiries and to get back to him. Then got out of the car and started walking.

He wandered for an hour or more, along the cobbled streets and up the stone steps to a couple of deserted properties. He found one that was a little larger, shaded by a vast fig tree, whose fruit lay rotting on the ground. The air thick with the scent of it but there was beauty in neglect, too; the paths were overgrown, the stone pool mossed and empty, but vivid cyclamen still burst from shaded pots and it wasn't Puerto Banus that was tempting him now.

'They're not interested in selling.' Charlotte soon got back to him. 'Especially not on a Sunday.'

'Get me a price,' Nico said, because there always

was one, and Nico was more specific with his instruction now, describing the house in detail, this the one that he wanted. He lingered a little longer, searching for answers to a question he didn't know, then back to the old town they went. Nico was looking for something he did not understand, but his head was pounding by the time he was back at the hotel.

He went to the bar.

Told himself it did not matter that there was no sign of her.

He checked his phone for perhaps the fiftieth time, answering it promptly when it rang. He was curiously deflated when it was Charlotte on the other end. Even Nico's eyes widened when his PA rang and gave him the price.

'He's not interested in negotiating,' Charlotte relayed.

'Who?' Nico asked.

'I just got a lawyer, and he wasn't particularly chatty. That's the price,' Charlotte said. 'Are you sure you're not in Monte Carlo?'

He let out a grudging laugh.

He worked well with Charlotte, perhaps because they rarely saw each other—she lived in London and was permanently available on the phone and online. Occasionally, when needed, she travelled with him, but their relationship had survived because, unlike too many previous PAs, Nico had not bedded her. Put simply there was no attraction, just mutual liking, and as a team they worked well.

'I'll ring and speak with him…'

'Well, good luck, but he's been instructed that you can take it or leave it. If you try to bring the price down, he will refuse to take any more calls.'

His business brain instantly rejected it, but for a moment he lingered. There was need to be here and he had no reason why.

His mind flicked to Constantine.

To dangerous thoughts of long-time lovers, but he hauled himself out of that tempting space.

But what if she needed somewhere to run to if she chose to reveal all?

Nico scolded himself for the very idea.

It was a bloody expensive women's refuge!

It would be a most fiscally unwise decision, logic warned him—he should follow his own rule, buy when the pendulum swung in the other direction, when the developer went bust or the rich and famous migrated to the next exclusive locale.

'I'll text you the number.' Charlotte said, but Nico halted her before she rang off.

'Tell him I'll take it and get the paperwork started.' He heard his voice disobey his brain's orders and then snapped off his phone.

Instinct won.

And then he looked up and saw her walk into the bar with her husband and their families. And she would be his lover, Nico decided. For her, he would break his rules—would be her regular refuge. He saw the strain on her features, saw her eyes almost pleading as they met his.

How she pleaded.

Connie felt like a hostage, her family her captor, and there, most unexpectedly, was Nico and she wanted his arms, wanted not to be made love to tonight but to be held, to be shielded, to be carried down the ladder from the wreckage her family had built for her.

She watched him stand.

Watched as he lifted his hotel key and rather pointedly pocketed it, and knew now that tonight she could go there—that Nico would be there for her, that maybe what she had wished for last night was being offered: liaisons in Athens; passion and phone calls; an occasional escape to a secret life.

How much easier it would be to play along with the charade, to laugh along with her parents and later say farewell to them, to turn into her hotel suite and then, a discreet while later, knock on Nico's door.

So badly she wanted to take the easy option—especially when it meant the sweet reward of Nico's arms tonight—but Nico had awoken something else within her, had made her a woman in more ways than he knew, for though scared she felt stronger.

It was for that reason she left Nico waiting alone through what would prove the longest night, in a bed that had been scented by them.

CHAPTER SIX

'I STILL can't believe you would do this to your father.'

She'd heard it a hundred, perhaps a thousand times, and it still stung as much as it had the first time, but Connie held her head high.

'I still can't believe that he would have done that to me.' She put the last of her things in her case, knew that her time here in Xanos was over for now. She had brought shame to the family—annulled the most celebrated marriage on the island—and there was no choice but to leave. The word was about to get out, the presents ready to be returned, the families confronted, the accusations and threats hurled, and through it all Connie had stayed calm, even when her father had, this very morning, collapsed with chest pain in his office and was, having been examined by the doctor, lying in his bed guarded by a nurse. When even that did not dissuade her, her mother had finally told her to get out. But now, as she tossed in a honeymoon dress that was still unworn and wrapped in unopened tissue paper, she thought of the excitement when she had bought it and she had to swallow down tears as she pulled the zipper closed on her case. The brave facade was slowly slipping.

They had been cruel in the face of her mutiny. Of course, she could make her own decisions, choose a different life—but if she lived here there were rules, and if she didn't…

Her bank accounts had been linked to the family business. All now were closed. Her car, which had been a present, had been taken back, all her jewellery, too. She was not to take the luggage, her mother said, that had been bought for her honeymoon. So she had fitted what she could into a very old case, appalled they would treat her this way, while deep down she had known all along this was how it would be.

'Your father worked so hard to give you everything. We are the richest in Xanos, the most respected, and you would destroy it, this how you treat him. This will kill him, Connie.'

It might.

Her father had played his trump card, lying in bed with chest pain, and, her mother savagely relayed, it would kill him should she still go ahead with the annulment. She should just get back in her box and be Stavros's wife.

'Let me see my father, explain to him…' Connie said as she had many times this morning.

'You've destroyed him, Connie,' her mother sneered. 'The doctor says he must rest, that there must be no more upset. Be a good girl for him and maybe he will get better.'

It would be so much easier to do.

But hadn't her father clutched at his chest throughout her teenage years—every time she'd questioned, every time she'd considered a different choice, every time she had dared to venture out? It had been the same thing and she couldn't live like this, couldn't be good for the rest of her life, just to avoid a funeral.

'I want a real marriage, Mum.' Surely she must understand it. 'Like you have. Can't you see that?' But it fell on deaf ears.

'How will it be for Dimitri, for poor Stavros? Did you ever stop to think about that?'

She couldn't stop thinking about it.

Even if he would have made the worst husband, her heart ached for Stavros, for both islands were the same in that respect—appearances, however false, were all that mattered to the island's elite. Far from hating Stavros, Connie felt sorry for him. He was as trapped as she would have been, forced to live a lie because that was what family dictated.

'If that's what he wants,' Connie's voice trembled, 'then Stavros will get another wife, poor woman.' She added, 'I just hope he has the guts to tell her this time before the wedding night.'

'Your father—'

Connie couldn't bear to discuss it even a moment longer. 'If you won't let me see him then I'll leave him a note.'

'If he lives to read it.' Her mother burst into tears again. She had dressed from head to toe in black since the day Connie had gone to their hotel room and told them she could not live this life. She had emerged from their row in this costume, as if someone *had* died, rather than that her daughter had stood up for herself. 'I'm going to lie down. You be gone when I get up.'

'You're not going to see me off?'

'Today you should be returning from your honeymoon.' She sobbed. 'Today should be my proudest day.'

It was the hardest note she had ever written.

Connie went to her father's study, which was the furthest room from her mother's wailing, and closed the heavy door. It was room that had both intimidated and intrigued her as child, all forbidden cupboards and locked drawers, and it intimidated her now, but quietly she roamed, trying to work out what to say in her letter.

The more they told her that she couldn't leave, the more she realised why she should.

Why absolutely she must.

Her hand moved to her stomach, and her mind moved to the question that had been begging for answer for days now.

She was late—just a day or two, but getting a pregnancy test on the island was impossible without causing gossip.

There were so many reasons for being late, Connie assured herself—the stress of the wedding and the aftermath.

After all, she had started on the Pill in readiness for her wedding. That might mess around with things.

But she hadn't been meticulous in taking it.

A baby would have been far from a disaster had her marriage been the one she had intended.

'Oh, God.' Panic assailed her, as it so often did these days. She took out the card from her purse, the card Nico had left on the breakfast bar, and how badly she wanted to speak to him, wanted to call him to take the help he had offered.

Not for the first time she dialled the number, and though Connie usually hung up before she had finished even dialling, so badly did she need support, someone who would understand the ways here and what she was dealing with, so badly did she want to hear Nico's voice, this time she let it ring. This time she listened and held her breath as he answered.

'Nico.' He said just this one word.

His voice was an abrupt version of the one she had previously heard—and she was reminded then of who she was dealing with. Not the man who had held her in his arms and made such wonderful love to her, not the man who had made her laugh and smile when she had never thought she would, but a shrewd businessman, a man who'd had many lovers, a man who set his sights on a goal and flew directly to it.

She knew for she had found out all she could about him since that night, had trawled the internet, had read about his success and the teary complaints from scorned lovers.

Their only complaint was that he had ended it, that Nico simply refused to even consider a relationship, or, as Nico called it, being tied down.

'Hello.' He spoke in English now, his voice harsh and a touch brutal and she drew in a sharp breath and rapidly hung up.

She could not speak to him, could not be the tearful, upset women again to him. She was better than that, Connie told herself. She was stronger than that.

She would get to the mainland and then, when she had got herself together, when she had found a job and somewhere to live, then, if necessary, she would call him.

And if not necessary, Connie thought with a smile, she might still call him!

Thank you. She said it in her head. She said it a thousand times a day, would not regret the potential of a life inside, not even for a second. In fact, it made her decision to leave easier.

There was no way her parents would accept what had happened .

She had, after all, qualified for an annulment given the marriage hadn't been consummated.

So she wrote the letter, said sorry for the pain she had caused, but truly hoped that one day her father would see she was right, that one day he could again be proud of her. Her third attempt and still she wasn't satisfied with it and Connie stood and wandered the room again, trying to find the words to tell her father that she loved him, but she had to live her own life.

Her hands explored the ornaments he collected, just as she had as a child, and then went to the drawers, just as she had as a child, too. As the catch gave, Connie realised that in all the drama and haste of her father's collapse and the doctor being called, for once her father had left things unlocked.

Connie checked each drawer, her heart in her mouth, terrified that her mother might come in and see what she was doing, but she was curious as to what he kept in there. There was nothing of much interest at first, just endless files, her father's meticulous notes.

And then she opened another drawer, a file marked 'Housekeeping' that she almost didn't bother looking into but she did. Almost immediately she wished she hadn't. The folder was thick and within was a file with some work for Dimitri, Stavros's father. She read of some less than legal deals her father had brokered for Dimitri, and the payments her father had received. Her eyes welled up as she realised the stellar island lawyer she had been taught to respect, the man who had been held up as shining example of all that could be achieved by honest hard work and study, was as much a criminal as the clients he at times defended.

Why would he keep this stuff? She went to close the folder, appalled at what she knew, but her first instinct for her father was to save him from the shame and disgrace if this ever came out.

'Eliades.'

The file caught her eye and the name burnt in her brain as she slammed closed the folder.

Eliades wasn't a particularly unusual name, Connie told herself. And her father would surely have no dealings with them, given they lived on Lathira. Nico's family would have lawyers and advisors of their own. They hadn't even spoken at the wedding. They were friends with Stavros's family, and, because she'd noticed Nico, she had noticed them but certainly hadn't seen them interacting with her family.

And yet she recalled showing her parents the guest list, and her father's face had frozen for a moment as he'd read who Stavros had intended to invite.

'Perhaps a smaller wedding…' Her father had attempted that night, but that was, of course, impossible. Their only child—of course the wedding had to be stupendous.

She wanted to close the folder, wanted to close the drawer, to forget what she knew, except another part of her wanted to know more.

It *was* Nico's family.

The papers were old and yellow and her heart seemed to lift to her mouth as she saw that her father had arranged Nico's adoption.

An illegal adoption.

She could feel her pulse in her temples, thought she might be the second in her family to collapse this morning as she realised the Eliades had bought a child.

Had bought Nico.

And it was her father who had sold him.

Did Nico even know he was adopted?

She saw the shaky handwriting of a woman, and

tried to see the surname, but could only make out the first name and it was Roula. Her eyes filled with tears when she saw the paltry sum the woman had been paid.

How could she contact Nico now? Connie asked herself. How could she face him, knowing what she knew and, worse, the part her father had played in it all?

Her mouth filled with saliva. For a moment she thought she might vomit, the room was so stifling. It was suddenly imperative that she sit down.

And then, as she turned over the piece of paper, Connie realised that she never, ever could contact him, for she was holding a birth certificate. Not the one that had been falsified to create a new identity—this gave the real date of birth, moved his age to a few months older and, far worse than that, there was another name.

Alexandros.

Nicolas had born eighteen minutes later.

In that moment, Connie knew that she had lost not just the man she loved but possibly the father to her baby.

CHAPTER SEVEN

'Well, if the baby's two months old, I don't see how the marriage could have been annulled. Clearly there were...' Everything had gone black then. Somehow Nico had maintained the phone conversation, had listened to his mother spout the latest gossip circling the two islands, had even managed to fire a few questions of his own in a voice that was presumably normal for his mother had not hesitated in her responses.

'She went to Athens, but Dimitri soon drove her out. She's in London now apparently...' his mother said in a loud, stage whisper, 'completely broke. Naturally, her parents cut her off when all the scandal happened... We'll see how long she lasts. No doubt she will return with her tail between her legs.'

'And Stavros?' Nico demanded.

'Stavros!' His mother forgot to whisper. 'Stavros left the island months ago—after that little tart shamed him. How could you not know that?'

Because they hadn't spoken in almost a year, Nico

could have pointed out to his mother, but he chose not to.

But what a year it had been.

He had flown from Xanos to Lathira after the wedding and walked into a blistering row of his own. Of course he wasn't adopted. His mother had laughed and pointed to his birth certificate, told him the proof was there in front of him.

'Where?' Nico had asked, for they had always been vague with details. 'Where was I born?'

'On the mainland. We moved here to start the new business.' And then, when Nico, unsatisfied with her responses, had requested DNA, she had screamed and raged and ranted, his father joining in, too. Only now, all these months later, had they started talking again, but it was back to talking about the weather. The real issue was too sore to be raised, no matter how many times he tried to.

And now he put down the phone to the news he could be a father.

Nico rested his head in his hands, tried to take the news in. His first instinct was to find and confront Constantine.

How could she not tell him? His first response was anger. She had his number, how dare she take away his right to know? Nico closed his eyes, dragged in a breath and wrenched that thought out, because it simply could not be.

He had sworn he would never be a father.

He was overreacting, he told himself. So what if a

woman he had slept with nearly year ago had had a baby? It didn't mean it was his. Anyway, Nico gave a cynical sigh, if it were his baby, there was no doubt in his mind that he would have been contacted long, long ago.

But, still, he wanted an answer, wanted perhaps to see her, to make sure for himself that she was all right, given all she must have been through. After a moment he had telephoned Charlotte, and it hadn't taken long. The ever-impressive Charlotte had drawn a blank at first, but when Nico had told her to say she was asking after Connie, rather than Constantine, phone numbers had led to more phone numbers, and then to a few employment agencies and now, a few hours and a plane trip later, he stood at dusk outside a large London home. The heavy iron gate dragged in the dirt and weeds as he pushed it open, sure, quite sure that the address must be the wrong one. The place looked uninhabited. Certainly he couldn't imagine Constantine living here, but he rang the bell and waited, then rang again, unsure what he was doing there. What he would he say if she did answer the door?

'Nico?' Had she not said his name, he would not have thought it was her.

She looked nothing like the woman he had met that day, nothing like the woman he had held that night.

She had put on weight, a lot of weight, her face was puffy and swollen, those gorgeous blue eyes peered out from two slits and that lush, ripe body was bloated now. Her once wild tumble of dark curls hung tired and lank and even that delicious mouth was dry and cracked, but it was not that which made her so unrecognisable, it was more her stance, the defeat in her as she opened the door as if all the fire, all the energy, all the passion that made her her had been extinguished.

And Connie was painfully aware of that.

She could see the shock in his features, the same shock she felt sometimes when she stared dull eyed at her reflection in the mirror and tried to reconcile what she saw with the woman she once had been.

She wanted to close the door, to hide—for never, ever would she want him to see her like this.

'You didn't call.' It was not the words he would have chosen to greet her with if he could do it again, but he had not rehearsed this. In fact, he had pondered all the way what he might say to her, and had decided he would see when he got there. 'I said, if ever you needed anything…' He looked her slowly up and down. 'And clearly you do…'

It was a touch brutal and again he wished he could retract his words as he saw her chin rise in defence.

'So sorry!' Connie snapped. 'Had you given me some warning, I'd have put on make-up, and answered the door in something a little more fetching…'

She missed the slight twitch of his lips as he realised not all of that energy in her had died. She missed it because an angry, sinewy voice came down the stairs and then several loud thumps as his stick hit the floor and Connie's heart raced again, for she was not allowed visitors. 'Connie,' the voice demanded, 'who is it?'

'Just a delivery,' Connie called, and then looked at Nico with urgent eyes. 'You have to go. I'm not allowed to entertain.'

'I'm not asking to be entertained,' Nico said,' just to talk.'

'I'm not allowed guests,' Connie said. 'Please, Nico, just go.'

'So what time are you off?' He saw her eyes screw closed, saw her shake her head and go to close the door, but he blocked it with his shoulder. 'When do you have a day off?'

'Please,' she begged. 'I don't get time off. I have to be on call…' She saw him frown, saw incredulity flicker across his gorgeous features and she just wanted him gone, did not want to be seen like this, but Nico just stood there. 'He's bedridden,' Connie explained. 'He needs someone here at all times.' Still Nico stood. And for a fleeting second she saw escape, that maybe Nico could help. Maybe she didn't have to tell him about her father. It was so wonderful to see him. His beauty, his presence she had never even for a moment forgotten, but somehow, to be kind perhaps, her mind had dimmed it; somehow she had convinced herself that he was surely not quite as stunning as she remembered. Yet here he was and she didn't want it to end. 'I'm going to the shops in the morning…' Connie attempted. 'Maybe we could meet for a few minutes for coffee.'

'A few minutes…'

He heard something else then, the wail of a baby, and clearly it irritated the old man, because the thumping on the ceiling became more insistent and he demanded that she shut up that noise.

And Nico was furious, incensed on both her and the infant's behalf, and he would not leave her there, not for a single night. There was no sensible thought pattern, no grandiose gesture. He just felt sick at what was taking place here, and he watched her eyes widen in horror as, without invitation, he pushed easily past where she held the door.

'You can't come in...' Connie whimpered, but he could, and Nico put a finger to his lips and stood in the hallway. Connie stood shaking, wondering how she could get rid of him without making a noise.

'Connie,' came the reedy voice, 'I need you...'

Nico's jaw tightened. He stood in the dingy hall of a home that must once have been beautiful but now smelt of neglect and old man. Constantine did not belong here and surely neither did the baby that was still wailing. 'I'm coming, Henry...' She turned to race up the stairs, but he caught her wrist.

'It sounds as if your baby needs you first.'

'And I'll tend to him soon,' she whispered, but she was terrified to leave her baby. She could see Nico was angry and assumed it was at her. What if he simply took him? What if, as she tended to Henry, he simply plucked her son from his from the crib and left?

His son.

Connie felt her breath tighten in her chest, could not leave her babe, yet could not dare keep Henry waiting, especially as the banging was nonstop now.

'Go to him,' Nico said in a low voice. 'I will wait here…'

'No.' She dared not trust him. She ran to the kitchen and scooped up her baby, and hushed him for a moment, but he was fretful as he nestled into her chest and heard his mother's hammering, panic-stricken heart. She fled up the stairs with him, then gently placed him on the carpet outside Henry's room where his screams intensified, but he was safer surely on the floor than in reach of a father who might choose to take him.

Henry was not best pleased. Connie had taken an hour off this afternoon to visit the doctor and he hated the baby that demanded his aide's attention, and the noise, he told her, as she repositioned his pillows and rubbed his back, was not acceptable. 'He'll be quiet soon,' Connie assured him. 'He needs feeding and then he'll settle.' Then she felt Henry's eyes linger on her heavy, aching breasts and she wanted to slap the disgusting old man, for his leers, for the endless silent innuendos, for the smile on his face as she washed him.

For so many things.

Except it was here or the street.

'I'll check on you later,' Connie said when Henry was settled, but still her baby wept.

'I'd like that.'

She did not respond, tried to ignore his veiled meanings, because, as she told herself so very often, he was all talk—but how she loathed it.

Loathed it so much her skin crawled in his presence, but she tried to look for the good in things. It was here she had worked through her pregnancy and Henry *had* hired someone to care for him for three weeks after a very difficult delivery and allowed her to stay there.

She picked up her babe and held him, closing her eyes against dizzy fatigue, and hoped against hope that the tablets the doctor had given her would work, that the cloud would soon lift and she could start creating a proper future for herself and her son.

'We'll get there,' she said to her tiny baby, holding him tight, but he would not be soothed. All he wanted was to be fed. 'Soon,' Connie hushed, because first there was a difficult conversation to have, an unexpected visitor to attend to, and, most importantly, Henry must have no idea she had allowed someone to enter his home.

Nico watched as she came down the stairs, holding the still crying baby, and she pressed her finger to her lips, warning him not to speak. She gestured for him to follow, which he did, down the long hallway to the rear of the house where she pushed open a large door. He found himself in a kitchen area, much brighter than what he had seen of the rest of the house. There was a certain homeliness to it—there was a crib and there was also a sofa decorated brightly with cushions.

She turned on the television and still she did not speak, placing the baby in his crib and trying to placate him with a dummy. She stacked and turned on the dishwasher and then turned the television up louder and only when there was enough noise filling the room to disguise their words did she speak.

'Please,' she begged. 'Keep your voice down.'

'I'm not the one making the noise,' Nico pointed out, because the baby had spat out his dummy and was again shrieking.

'I need to feed him.'

'Then feed him,' Nico said. 'I'll make a drink.' He found his way about the kitchen as the woman he had spent but a few hours with picked up her child and sat on the sofa and started to feed her babe.

It was not as awkward as she expected, just a relief to finally sit and feed him, to let her brain catch up with the turn of events as Nico boiled the kettle and read the instructions on a jar of instant coffee.

'A teaspoon,' Connie said, 'and two of sugar.'

'It looks revolting,' Nico commented, because he had never had instant coffee before and certainly not the powdered home brand that was available to him now.

'Don't talk about my friend like that,' Constantine said, because coffee was possibly her only friend at the moment. It was her saviour at two a.m. and again at four, and it woke her up in the mornings, and now, after this one, she could tackle the mountain of washing both Henry and the baby created. She watched Nico's lips move into a small smile as he got her wry humour.

He was really rather patient, making her a drink and letting her feed her baby in gentle silence for a little while. Patient was something she would never have expected a man like Nico to be in a circumstance such as this.

She had read more about him, of course, since then.

A man who jetted around Europe and America, a man of many lovers and deals, he bristled with restless energy and yet, as she fed the baby, he sat on a barstool and sipped on his coffee. Then he looked, not in an embarrassed or awkward way because she was feeding, he just looked straight into her eyes and his voice when it came seemed to reach into her soul, because he was the first person to ask without accusation, the first person to want to hear her version of events.

'What happened?'

And she hesitated, because she honestly hadn't had time to assess—the stocktake of her life had been put into the too-hard basket as she'd merely struggled to survive. Now this beautiful man sat in someone else's kitchen, and though he must have demands and difficult questions, he did not ask the one she had dreaded most, he did not refer to their son. He just looked to her and after a moment her answer came.

'I don't know.' She waited for a caustic comment, for a mental slap in return for her vagueness, but still he just sat. 'I don't know how I got to this point.' She closed her eyes for a moment, felt her child suckle her breast, and was so grateful for that, that even if her milk supply was drying up, for now she could feed him. She loved the moments together where the world disappeared and it was just the two of them, but always she was forced to return.

'You asked for an annulment?'

Constantine's eyes jerked up, realising he wanted the full story, and close to a year ago seemed like a lifetime now. It had been a very different life she had led since then, and she'd been a very different person then, too.

'I couldn't stay married.' Connie said. 'I simply couldn't...' And unlike her parents, unlike Stavros, unlike the priest, the lawyer, the maids, everyone, he did not roar or cry or beg or weep or explode, he just accepted her words. 'I told them that night...' She looked for his reaction, but he gave none. 'The night I saw you in the bar...'

He gave nothing away, did not tell her how long that night had been, of the disappointment he had felt, the regret of waking in an empty bed, or that he had offered her more than he had any other woman.

Instead he waited for her.

'They didn't take it well.'

'I can imagine.'

'I don't think so.'

'I know what families are like on the islands.'

And for a moment she conceded.

'My mother...' He hesitated after using that word, but he did not change it. 'She said at first you had moved to Athens...'

Wearily she nodded. She had been too busy to stop and think of that terrible time, and it was exhausting even now to remember it. 'I found a job, but it turned out that Dimitri knew the owner, or rather he made it his business to find out who he was and discredit me...' Connie's voice was flat. 'Everything I touched turned to nothing, every door that opened slammed closed as soon as people knew my name. I was told when I left that Dimitri would do his best to destroy me…' She gave a defeated shrug. 'I guess they were right.'

'They are cruel and fight nasty when they believe they have been slighted,' Nico said, because his parents had once attempted the same with him, doing their best to halt any opportunity that presented itself, doing everything they could to get him to return. 'What did you do?'

'I had enough money to get to London. I thought I would have more chance here given that no one knew me, but my parents cut me off completely, the money I had soon ran out…' She gave a tense swallow. 'My pregnancy was starting to show…' And she did not even attempt to explain it, for this he could not understand— no man could understand the fear of being pregnant with nothing and no one to fall back on. A fear not for yourself but for the life growing inside you.

He fought down the instinct to pounce, to ask the inevitable, because a deeper instinct told him now was not the time. He could feel her exhaustion, knew the terse, heated debate that it surely would be, and it was not fair to her to have it now.

She was in not fit state and it could wait, Nico told himself, for facts were facts, and, whoever the father, that would not change.

Still the question burnt within him and she could not know that he sat and wrestled with himself.

It must wait, Nico told himself, because, despite his ruthlessness at times, he only ever fought with equals, and at the moment she was weak.

'This was the only job I could get,' Connie continued as the unvoiced question remained unanswered. 'I needed something that came with accommodation.' She closed her eyes in shame, because this was never how she wanted to be seen. 'And it was somewhere to come home to after the birth…' She faltered for a moment because, of all the terrible times, that had been the worst. Giving birth in a busy hospital, feeling so alone and frightened, and it had been a complicated, difficult delivery. All she could hear at the end had been Nico's name, for she had been screaming for him.

That he did not need to know.

All she had to show him was that she would be okay. 'I am getting things sorted,' she said. 'Soon, in a few weeks, I will start applying for better jobs, once I have sorted out a creche and a flat.' Her voice quivered at the enormity of all she faced. With no references, no money, how on earth could she support her child?

'You don't have to worry about money. I will—'

'Oh, please…' Far from comforting her, his words actually terrified her. She didn't want him to have a hold on her, didn't want to be tied to a man who, by his own admission, wanted neither a wife nor children. Her one brief foray into marriage had been a clear disaster. As for her relationship with Stavros, while in it, she had thought it bearable, had assumed that was how people lived, but looking back it had been hell. Her self-esteem was shot from the constant rejections and less than veiled criticisms. She wanted her child to have an independent, strong mother, and she would work her way towards being that, and certainly she could not imagine him, so sleek and elegant, sharing access to her son. 'I want to make my own way. I want to support him myself.'

'It's not just about you!'

'I don't want you in my life.' It came out all wrong, but so adamant were the words, so strong the effect that for a moment Nico was silent.

He could feel acid churn in his stomach. It was all very well for her to choose to live like this, but he would not allow it for… He stopped himself from voicing it, even in his head. For now he would try to sort this by removing dangerous emotion, by not even thinking that the baby might be his. He would treat her for now, Nico decided, as he would a client, be objective as he dealt with the issues she faced. 'Let's just concentrate on getting you out of here. Are you managing to save?' Always practical, he tried to steer her to a solution. Perhaps if he could help her get a flat, arrange some child care, at least get on her feet, then, maybe then, they could talk, but his question went unanswered and a frown formed as he saw her swallow. 'What are you paid?' He did not care if the question was rude.

'I have accommodation, and I have food,' Connie said, not revealing that she ate the same as Henry did, that the disgusting porridge and mince and potato was all that was available. 'In return I look after his home…'

'He doesn't pay you?'

'A little.' Constantine revealed the paltry sum that hardly covered the nappies, that gave her no option but to breastfeed, and her milk was already starting to dry up.

Nico closed his eyes and took a deep breath for a moment, and it was game over.

He could not treat her as a client.

'It's the twenty-first century…' His voice rose and she begged him quiet, but he lowered it only slightly. 'You cannot be treated like a slave. There are people who deal with single mothers, with wages…'

'And I have qualifications and a wealthy family back home in Greece,' Connie retorted, for she had looked into that. 'I'm hardly a priority. There are people far worse off than me.' It was hard at times to remember that. 'I'm getting things sorted.' She was, she meant it. She was doing everything in her power to ensure a better future for her child, to lift herself out of the hole she was in. 'I went to the doctor today, he gave me vitamins and some tablets. Once they kick in…'

'Tablets?'

'He says I have postnatal depression.' She watched his eyes narrow. 'I didn't want to take anything while I was feeding, but he said they were safe.'

'I'd have postnatal depression if I lived here.' He wasn't being derisive, absolutely he wasn't. 'You are not depressed, Constantine, you are miserable because you are exhausted. Tablets won't help that.'

'Oh.' She gave a tired laugh, absolutely devoid of humour. 'I'll take what I can get.'

A banging on the ceiling had Nico's jaw clamp down,

and it ground tighter as he saw the baby murmur a tired protest as she moved him from her breast.

'He's still feeding,' Nico said as she stood. Breastfeeding did not embarrass him, it was that she might interrupt this time to tend to the demands of the greedy man upstairs that caused the gruffness to his voice.

'He's asleep,' Connie said, but even though he was, she knew she had stolen some precious food from her son. Henry was still banging, so she sorted out her clothing and without a word headed upstairs.

'What's all the noise?' Henry demanded. 'Who's down there?'

'No one. I'm sorry,' Connie attempted. 'I had the television too loud. Can I get you a drink?'

'Just my pillows.'

She hated sorting his pillows most, and it was the thing he most often asked. How she hated leaning him forward and arranging the pillows, knowing where his eyes were, where his cheeks were.

Had Nico been able to see the smile on Henry's face at that moment, instead of Connie laying the old man back down, he'd have been laying him out, but for now he sat in the quiet kitchen, trying to work out how best to handle things.

He had not stopped to think since he'd heard the news—after finding where she was he had pretty much stepped on a plane and now he had to sort something out.

Thankfully the baby was sleeping. Nico did not go

over and look. It was almost as if he did not want to
see, to know, to have it confirmed.

Deal with the issue.

It was his mantra and it never failed him.

In crises at work, he simply silenced the voices, cut
through the tape and dealt with what was, not what
might be, not what had been, but what was.

Constantine, for now, was the issue.

If it was not his son… He looked around the kitchen,
heard her footsteps walking above and knew that even
if the baby were not his, he couldn't simply walk away.

And if it was… Nico sat still for a long moment,
wrestled with indignation, with the betrayal at not being
told, which led to more anger against a woman who
wanted to go alone, so he clamped his mind closed on
those issues and fought to get to the vital point. If this
was his child, what then?

She did not want him in her life.

His mind raced for an instant solution.

Declare her unfit?

Take the child?

To what?

For what?

Raw was his honesty.

His lifestyle was lavish, he ate out most nights,
hopped on planes, and the only thing he had to think
about changing was the time on his watch.

He looked at the dark hair on the back of the child's
head, to the white sheet over his shoulders, and it was
a relief not to see his face, safer by far not to love him.

Love did not last. Something deep inside told him that.

'You must go.' Constantine was at the door.

He should, Nico realised. He should get up now and let her continue her miserable life and get on with his—except he could not leave it there.

'Come with me.'

She gave a tired smile, but Nico wasn't joking.

'I mean it,' Nico said. 'Come back to my hotel.' He saw her eyes shutter, no doubt thinking he was about to add to her exhaustion. 'Separate rooms,' he added.

Which just made her feel worse. Oh, she wasn't up for a sexual marathon, but for him to so quickly discount her…

'I'm not your problem.'

The baby might be, but he did not want to broach that, so he tried another approach. 'I feel that I engineered this, that you would be married to Stavros if it were not for me.'

'And I'd no doubt be feeling exactly the same,' Connie pointed out, 'with my little IVF baby and a husband that couldn't stand to touch me—a little less tired perhaps, but still on the happy pills!' She hated this, hated to be seen like this. Pride was her downfall, because she could beg and weep to her family, could go online tomorrow and tell the world how she was living and shame would move her family to bring her home, but she would not force charity. 'It would be just as bad…'

'It could not be as bad,' Nico refuted. 'It could not be worse.'

There were unexpected prices for pride, and she paid one now—because here was the man who had seen her so beautiful. Here was the man she escaped to in weary snatched dreams, looking more beautiful than she had dared ever remember, yet she had seen the shock in his eyes when she had opened the door, the bewildered start as he'd realised the swan had reverted, and now he was seeing her at her very worst.

'If I had led you back to your room instead of mine, if I had not said those things about choices…'

'I'm glad that you did.' Her admission surprised even her, but now she thought about it, now she looked at how her life would have been without Nico's intervention that night, despite all her problems, it was still here that she would rather be. She felt better for him being there, better for their talk, better now that she could see more clearly, and spirit rose within her. 'Things aren't great now,' she admitted. 'I know there will be struggles ahead, but I will get there.'

And there was still a glimmer of fire in her tired, dull eyes, and Nico was in no doubt now that with or without him she would.

'This is temporary,' Connie said, her voice firmer now. 'Had I stayed I would have felt like this forever.'

'Why didn't you call?' Nico asked the question he had when he had first arrived at her door, for he had given her his private number that morning at breakfast. Even then he had been worried to leave her.

'Why didn't you?' Connie asked. She could never tell him the real reason so she went on the defensive instead—after all, he would have surely heard from his family the scandalous outcome to the wedding. Why should it be her that picked up the phone? Had he cared, even a jot, if their one night together had meant even a fraction of what it had to her, surely he could have called in those days and weeks as the news broke, just to see that she was okay. That he had not spoke volumes.

The only reason he was here was because of the child and she must remind herself of that.

He was here for his son, nothing else.

'I did not hear about this till today,' Nico said. 'The moment I found out I had my PA track you down and I got on a plane.'

'Oh, please,' Connie retorted, because she knew how big the news had been, that even if he only made occasional visits and duty phone calls to his family, he would have been told. 'As if your family wouldn't have gossiped about this—'

'We were not talking for a long time—only in recent weeks have we spoken,' Nico interrupted. 'After your wedding…' Only the slightest pause gave indication that this subject was a painful one. 'There was a falling out—a large one. Only in the last few weeks have we started speaking again. I have had a difficult year.'

Not that difficult, Connie wanted to say, because he stood tall and strong and beautiful; he was every bit the man she had left. 'Too difficult to pick up the phone?'

And he never shared private matters and he wasn't particularly comfortable in doing so now, but better that than her to think he had known and not thought to contact her. 'I found out they were not my parents.'

Connie stood frozen—not at the news, because she had found out the same already, but that he knew and that Nico would tell her. She was shocked he would share what surely no one else knew, because if that news got out it would make her annulment and pregnancy idle chatter.

'How?' It was husky, and the word stuck in her throat. Did he know already that her father was involved? Was that, in fact, why he was here?

'I remembered.' He said it so simply. His voice did not betray the pain and the heartache, the jumble of feelings and dreams that made, almost, a memory. 'I'm wrong apparently. My parents deny...' His voice trailed off. He was not here to talk about himself and not used to sharing.

'Tell me,' Connie offered, because pain had entered the building, and now that he was not looking at her, now that he focussed instead on the television behind her, she could really look at him. Yes, the year had left its mark on him, too. He was a touch thinner perhaps, but that was not it. She tried to fathom what the change was, but couldn't.

He shook his head, because he had said more than enough already, and Connie did not push again, scared what her tired brain might reveal in an unguarded moment.

'You'd better go.'

He had better.

He could leave what he had in his wallet, and if she threw it at him, then she could pick it up later. He could send her regular cheques each month and it was up to her if she cashed them. He could go, safe in the knowledge that soon she would be strong, but there was a scent in the kitchen that had him linger, the sweet smell of baby. Then he looked over at her and thought how much better he could make things.

Not forever, he quickly told himself, because there could be no forever, his heart had learnt that long ago.

But he could expedite things, get her back on her feet sooner, help set her up with somewhere decent to live, but for now she needed to rest and get strong and, he admitted, albeit reluctantly, she simply deserved a little looking after. 'Come with me,' Nico said, and this time he meant it. 'Not to the hotel, but back to my home. I will hardly be there, you can rest, get your strength, I have staff…'

'I'll be fine.' She meant it, she absolutely meant it—she just hadn't quite worked out how.

'Come with me.' He said it again. 'I have a property on Xanos—the south.'

She gave a wry laugh, had this vision of blondes draped over his white loungers, of million-dollar views and champagne cooling, and could not be the ragamuffin guest. 'I'm not interested,' Connie said. 'I'm trying to get away from my family—I hardly want to go back to Xanos.' It was Connie frowning now. 'I didn't know you had property there.'

'No one knows,' Nico said. 'It is very private, extremely secluded. There is a stretch of beach that is mine and you can walk undisturbed there. There is a pool and a garden where you can get back some colour...' He looked at her tired pale cheeks and his mind was made up. 'I have a housekeeper who cooks with local produce.'

'Your staff will soon talk.'

'My staff were hand-picked.' He saw her dismiss that. After all, she knew how the island worked, that the people thrived on gossip—it was a factor he had considered on hiring Despina and Paulo. 'They are an elderly couple,' Nico explained. 'Proud people, who lost their only son a couple of years ago—all their savings had gone into his health. They have nothing. The developer bought their home and was charging them the most ridiculous rent. Now they live in a property to the rear of mine and they tend to the house and garden as if it were there own.' He looked over at Constantine and would not for a moment let her compare him to Henry. 'I pay them not just their board but a good wage, too— my staff have dignity, and that brings loyalty. I insist on privacy. No one, not even my family, knows that I am there.'

'Why?' Connie blinked. 'Why the secrecy?'

He had no choice but to tell her. If she came she'd find out anyway, for there were papers everywhere and records that he pored over whenever he got a chance. 'I am from there,' Nico said. 'I am sure of that. I want to find out my past...' And she felt her blood run cold as he continued, 'So for now, in my free time, I base myself in Xanos.'

'Doing what?'

'Searching,' Nico said. 'I want to find out who and where my parents are.'

'And then…' Connie was having great trouble finding her voice. 'Once you've found them, you'll…' She struggled, tried to stop herself from asking too many questions, but she wanted to be sure that was all he wanted, wanted to know that her family would be safe. Nico didn't wait for her to finish her stumbling sentence. He cut straight in and she saw then what she hadn't been able to place before, recognised then the change in him and it was anger. 'I don't just want to find them. I want to find out who facilitated this, and, when I do—' how black were his eyes as he continued, how badly they bored into her heart '—they will pay.'

CHAPTER EIGHT

THEY *would* pay.

Connie was quite sure of it.

He would ruin her family, of that she had no doubt. The shame she had wreaked on them would be nothing, *nothing* compared to what Nico would do when he found out the truth.

All of the truth, for she knew more.

She had seen the papers, had held them in her hands, and knew there was much more to this than parents giving up their baby.

'Get your things,' Nico said, and she was about to say no, but maybe she was too tired to process things properly. Perhaps by being there she could prevent him from finding things out because, Connie knew, the outcome could only be devastating. 'We leave now.'

'I can't,' Constantine said. 'I can't just leave Henry...'

'He treats you like a slave.'

'He's an old man,' Connie said. 'And slave labour or not, I signed up for the job.'

'Then you leave in the morning.'

'I doubt the agency can get a replacement any time soon.'

'Oh, they will,' Nico said darkly.

'I can't…' She wanted to go; there was a part of her that was tempted to just escape, to go home, to hide at his property and heal, and there was part of her too that needed to be there, to stop the train wreck that would surely happen. But there was another reason that she was scared to go.

One reason.

And Nico knew it and he faced it.

'We need to talk,' Nico said. 'There are things we need to discuss.' He looked at her lank hair, her puffy face, could feel the exhaustion that seeped from her, and his harsh voice softened. 'But not now,' he said, 'not yet—not till you are ready.' He saw hope flare in her dull eyes as he tossed her the lifeline, and he willed her to take it. 'You have my word. For now all you have to do is deal with the basics.'

'The basics?'

'Be a mother,' Nico said. 'And when you're not being a mother, you rest.'

How sweet those words were, how tempting, how blissful it sounded. She wanted to close her eyes right now, to just sink into them, not think of problems, the hows, the whys, the hell that surely would follow.

She wanted what he offered.

'Rest,' Nico said. 'We'll leave in the morning. For now you should sleep.' But Connie shook her head.

'I have to do the laundry.' He watched as she heaved

a basket across the kitchen and he saw her jaw tighten as, instead of offering to help, he sat down, and just once as she loaded filthy sheets into the machine did she glance up, but said nothing.

And still she said nothing as she turned the machine on, and then opened the dryer, pulling more of the same out and folding the old man's bedding, but he could feel her tension at his lack of assistance as he picked up the remote and flicked the television to the news.

'I don't do laundry,' he said.

'Clearly,' Connie said as she dragged out the ironing board.

'You want to be a martyr...' He shrugged. 'Go ahead.'

And she didn't want to be a martyr so, for the first time, rather than ironing them, she put away the board and she just folded them instead.

'Rebel,' Nico said, glancing up, and she felt something she hadn't in a very long time—a move on the edge of her lips that was almost a smile as she left the wretched laundry and sat on the only seat left in the kitchen, the one on the sofa beside him. It was horribly awkward, staring ahead at the news when she wanted to turn and stare at him, wanted to talk, but scared what might come out if she did.

'Why don't you go to bed?' Nico suggested. 'While he sleeps, shouldn't you rest?'

'I shall go to bed as soon as you've gone.'

'Oh, I'm going nowhere,' Nico said. 'I'm not giving

you a chance to come up with a million reasons why you can't leave in the morning. I'm staying right here.'

'What about your hotel room? What about—?'

But Nico wasn't going to argue. 'Go to bed.'

And she sat there.

'Go on,' he said, and her face burnt, and she bit back tears. Neither victim nor martyr did she want to be, but dignity was sometimes hard to come by.

'You're sitting on it.'

And to his credit he said nothing, did not act appalled, just headed over to the kitchen and prepared the second cup of instant coffee he had ever had in his life, then perched himself on the barstool.

'There is a bedroom.' She felt the need to explain. 'It's just Henry moans if...' she hesitated a moment '...the baby starts crying. He can't hear so much if we are down here.'

And there was the longest pause so he was determined not ask, but more than that, he wanted to know. 'What's his name?'

'Leo,' Connie said, and swallowed, because by tradition he should be Vasos after Nico's father, and though she had ached to name him Nico, it would have been too much of a constant reminder, so instead she had named him Leo, for it was in August that he had been made.

'Sleep,' he ordered, and she unravelled a blanket.

And she tried to sleep.

Turned her back on him and faced the faded pattern

of the sofa, tried not to think about the man in the room and that tomorrow she would leave here with him.

Tried not to fathom her scary future.

Because, even with Nico's offer, the future was scary. Scarier, in fact, than going it alone, because the truth would out—deep down she knew that.

She was just in no position to run from it.

CHAPTER NINE

SURPRISINGLY, she slept.

Despite his presence, despite her anxiety about the next day, with Nico in the room, a strong, quiet presence, somehow her exhausted mind stilled. Somehow she fell asleep to the whir of the tumble dryer and washing machine and did not think about what the next day would bring.

Even in the night, when her baby awoke, Constantine hardly did. Nico watched in silence as, surely more asleep than awake, she dragged herself from the sofa at Leo's first murmur, crossed the dark room and changed her child then went back to the sofa with him. She curled on her side, hardly a word spoken, just a hush to her baby and then the sound of him feeding, and after a while, when the room was silent, he watched her sleep-walk her baby back to his crib. It happened again early in the morning, but this time the feed was interrupted by the incessant demands of the old man.

'I could go up for you?' Nico offered, the third time she dashed to the stairs.

'And scare the life out of him.'

He was more tempted than she could know, but he held onto his temper. Nico even sat quietly while Constantine rang the employment agency, watching her fingers rake through her long hair as she explained that today she would be leaving.

'Next week?' Connie said, and Nico's jaw tightened and she knew, just knew, he was about to take the phone from her, but she was determined to handle this. 'I want someone here today.' But the agency knew Connie was a responsible woman who would not leave the old man alone, and took full advantage of that fact. For, really, they could find someone at their leisure without her walking out. Defeated, she handed him the phone.

'Nico Eliades speaking.' His voice was one she had heard before, that morning she had rung him from her father's study.

Formal.

Brutal.

'You have one hour to send someone or, failing that, to get here yourself.' And he said a little more than that, as Connie sat cringing, that he was considering reporting them. First he would check with his lawyers about minimum wage and work hours, and most certainly he would do that at ten a.m., 'if no one is here'.

The owner was there within half an hour.

She told Henry, who must have been used to staff leaving, because he didn't seem remotely bothered. He knew full well there would be plenty of others who were desperate to take her place.

Connie packed her things into her suitcase, which bulged a little more now that it had to hold Leo's things.

'What about the crib?'

'It was already here.'

'Then let's go.'

He took the case she had been struggling with and held it as easily as if it were an empty carrier bag and then handed it to a driver who was coming to the door.

'Are we going back to the hotel?' she asked as she climbed into the car. He had thought of everything, Connie realised, because there was even a baby seat. Or rather he had informed his driver, because Connie really couldn't imagine him fitting it, and certainly he offered no help as for the first time she wrestled with straps and the buckle and fitted Leo into the seat.

'I don't know how it goes.' She was embarrassed after a couple of attempts and he sat in the seat beside her, clearly wanting to get going and unused to this type of delay.

'Don't look at me,' Nico said, and drummed his fingers on the car door as he sat impatiently waiting for the click that told them Leo was safely secured.

It was only as they drove off, as her life changed forever again, that Connie realised not once had he so much as looked at their baby.

CHAPTER TEN

'IT's beautiful.' It was her first glimpse of Xanos in almost a year and, even if she had never seen the south, it looked like home. Certainly it was a relief to almost be there.

Though luxurious, the journey had been long, especially with a fretful baby and milk that just wasn't flowing.

Connie had been tempted to ask if they could stop at a chemist when they hit the mainland so she could buy some provisions in case her milk ran out, but was too embarrassed to have such a discussion with Nico. Instead, she stayed quiet as they transferred to a small seaplane. As Xanos came into view, her tiredness lifted a little at the sight before her, great sweeps of beach that broke up the bright blue ocean and then gave way to lush, green hills. Though it was her island, Connie had never visited this side, let alone from a seaplane. From the air it was completely stunning.

She knew there had been many grumbles as to the size of the development but she had never really comprehended just how big it was. Now, as they drew closer, Connie could see the lavish houses with their infinity pools. There was a large hotel that Nico pointed out, called Ravels, and her throat tightened with the thought of living amongst all the finery.

Her family was considered wealthy by old Xanos standards, but their wealth was nothing, *nothing* compared to this, and frankly it was all rather intimidating.

'This,' Nico said as the plane made a perfect landing and glided smoothly to a small jetty, 'is where sometimes you will get wet. Depending on the tide,' he explained, but the tide was behaving today. The pilot unloaded both her and Nico's luggage, Connie's a rather sad-looking affair beside his smart black cases. There was one tricky moment: the pilot had placed a small ramp for her to walk on and she wanted to turn, to ask for Nico to take her baby while she negotiated it and then for him to pass Leo to her, but even as she turned her head to ask, she changed her mind. Nico made his feelings perfectly clear on that subject with his choice of words.

'Pass him to the pilot. Then he can take your hand and help you.'

The pilot did help, handed her back Leo, then went ahead with their cases as Connie walked at a rather slower pace along the jetty and then onto the sandy beach, revelling in the feel of the Xanos sun on her skin again, and scents she hadn't known she'd missed but which turned out to be blissfully familiar. The salty smell of the ocean filled her hungry lungs, and even if it wasn't to her parents', she felt a little as if she were coming home, bringing Leo for the first time to a place where he belonged.

'It used to be considered the poor side,' Connie said. 'But not now.' She looked as luxury cars sped along the narrow road. She looked at the hotel and a large balcony where she could just make out diners enjoying the early evening sun. They walked just a little further, little Leo growing heavy in her arms, and as they stepped off the beach she decided she was getting rather too used to Nico's lavish ways because she was sure a driver would appear to take them the rather long walk to the development. Quite sure, in fact, that the pilot would have their bags already loaded in an undoubtedly luxurious car.

Except there was no car, just an empty stretch of street, the pilot walking out through a stone arch on the other side of the road and nodding to Nico.

'All inside for you, sir.'

Nico thanked him and, to her surprise Nico led her through the stone archway and into a garden that was a real one. The noise of low water fountains greeted her, as did a full, glittering stone pool and there was nothing intimidating about it. It was nothing like she had imagined Nico owning, for this was no glittering modern property. Instead, it was a glorious old whitewashed home with an elderly couple waiting at the doorway to greet them. The only sign that it was Nico's home was a low sports car parked to the side of the house, and as

Nico saw her look at it he offered her the use of it any time he was at work.

Connie was quite sure she wouldn't drive it!

'Despina.' Nico introduced an elderly lady who, unlike Connie's mother, was dressed in black for real reasons. She practically fell on Leo, asking if it was okay for her to have a hold. It was a relief to hand him over, to let Despina take him, as her husband, Paulo, shook Nico's hand and then pointed out the changes that he had made to the garden in the week or two that Nico had been away. It wasn't just the weight of the baby in her arms that lifted, but a vast weight from her shoulders as she was ushered inside by Despina, leaving Paulo to work in the garden. It was how it should have been for Leo with her parents, Connie thought. This the welcome home that he deserved.

'Go and wash and change,' Despina said, 'and then I have ready your dinner.' She showed her to a room that was simple. Despina was still holding Leo as Connie looked around. There was a wooden bed, with crisp Greek linen and lace, and shutters on the window, and, amazingly, there was already a cot put up. Even if it was being silly, Connie felt a little uncomfortable, wondering if it was Despina's dead son's crib. There were many superstitions on the island that she'd grown up with, but Despina soon put her at ease. 'My niece just moved—they are away for a year with her husband and children. She is happy for you to use her things.'

'That's so kind of you.' Connie was touched at the thought that had gone into all this, and then, just as she was about to go, Leo started crying and Connie had to feed him. 'It's every two hours…' She closed her eyes in exhaustion. 'I don't think he's getting enough.'

How nice it was that Despina was patient, that she sat with Connie as she attempted to feed, but Leo kept crying and Connie was getting more agitated. 'I think it might be the travel and everything,' Connie admitted. It was such bliss to have someone wise to talk to, to confide in, another woman who had been there before and done it.

'I bought some formula and bottles when Nico said you were bringing a baby. It's all there in the kitchen.'

'I still want to feed him.'

'Maybe now you can rest, things will get better, but if he is waking so much at night…' She gave a shrug. 'It's there just in case. For now have your shower.' Despina said. 'I will watch him.'

It was bliss to have a shower and for the first time not have to listen out for Leo, knowing he was safe in Despina's arms. She washed her hair, too, felt the last of London slide down the plughole, and then she combed it through and washed out the clothes she had been wearing for tomorrow. Then she went to her bedroom where Despina had placed a now sleeping Leo in his cot and Connie opened her case—the decision what to wear was not a difficult one. Certainly she wished she had more choice, but she settled for leggings and a long swing top that had seen her through most of her pregnancy and the weeks after the birth.

She wasn't particularly nervous to go for dinner,

Despina had made her so welcome, but as Connie stepped into the living area, she saw the small kitchen was empty. The table was laid and Nico was sitting on the lounge, talking on the phone, and she realised they were alone.

'Where's Despina?' she asked when the phone had clicked off.

'Home,' Nico said. 'There is a smaller house to the rear of the property. I think I mentioned it before. Despina takes care of the cleaning and meals if I require them. Paulo keeps an eye on the garden.'

'Oh.'

'It's all a bit basic…' His hand swept around the simply furnished home. 'Though not for much longer. There are some designs in progress. I am trying to purchase the land to the side of the property, once that is in place the rebuild will start.'

'It's lovely as it is,' Connie said, because absolutely it was, certainly better than the palatial penthouse she had been nervously anticipating, but Nico just shrugged, clearly less than impressed with the place.

'I have asked Despina to come over more while you are here, to help with the baby…'

'I don't need help with Leo.' Her response was immediate, because as gorgeous as it had been to have ten minutes to herself, she did not need help taking care of her son.

'She can make your bed, then.' He dismissed her protests. 'Prepare your meals.'

'I can cook!' Connie said, 'I'm not an invalid, I don't

need someone cooking and cleaning for me. In fact...'
she had an idea that would perhaps make her feel less
beholden to him '...why don't I take care of the house
while I'm here?'

'To save me the money I pay Despina?'

His voice dripped sarcasm, and also Connie realised quickly just how stupid that idea was. She hardly
wanted to do the woman out of a job. 'I mean, to give
her a break, perhaps...'

'Fine,' Nico said. 'I'll cancel her.' He shrugged.
'There is a small boat that leaves at eight each morning, it takes you to the market. Might be a bit tricky
with Leo and all those bags, I saw the trouble you had at
the jetty.' She thought for a moment as she stood there,
blushing at her own stupidity. Despina wasn't just nice,
she was a necessity, but Nico hadn't finished teasing her
yet. 'But if you can't manage the boat, perhaps you can
eat at the taverna,' he suggested, his tongue firmly in
cheek. 'It would be a bit too far to walk to Ravels with
Leo.'

'I doubt they welcome babies.' She could be as sar-
castic as Nico when she chose to be.

'So,' Nico said, 'Despina stays. And you will not of-
fend my housekeeper dragging a mop around yourself
or folding sheets. You are to rest, to relax, recover from
the birth and then...' Black eyes met hers but thankfully
he did not complete what he was saying, stuck to his
promise that for now any difficult topics were on hold,
but it was all there in his eyes, and it was there, too, in
the knot deep in her stomach. She was terrified of his

reaction, not just to fatherhood but when he found out what her father had done. 'For now,' Nico said, 'we eat.'

It was the dinner she had dreamed of.

Every night as she'd made Henry's stew and mashed potato and then sat down much later to the same meal for herself, she had wished for this.

Slivers of lamb tossed in tzatziki, and a salad of thick slices of tomato drizzled in Xanos's olive oil, and surely there were no better olives? Connie closed her eyes as she bit into one, could taste the lemon and garlic they had been marinated in. It was a simple dinner, but completely the tastes she had grown up on and Nico watched as she relished each bite.

'What?' She blushed as she caught him watching her.

'It's good to see you enjoying it.' He poured himself a glass of wine, but when he offered, Connie shook her head.

'No, thanks.' She took a drink of water and relished it. 'The water is so much fresher and softer here. I am enjoying my dinner,' she admitted, and then she admitted a little more. 'It's not what I thought it would be. I mean, even as we flew in, I assumed we'd be going to the newer homes, or perhaps to the hotel.'

A year ago, they would have been.

Even a few months ago, that would have been the case.

But after employing the elderly couple to sort out the chaos of the neglected old house, on each trip back to Xanos, when he needed to go through papers, to make calls and go through records, though initially he had stayed at Ravels, each time he had visited he had stopped by at the house. He stayed for dinner when Despina suggested it, then dinner had stretched to staying a night now and then, and now it had been weeks since he had graced Ravels.

'It is more private here,' Nico said, but did not offer more. Did not tell her the unexpected pleasure in choosing wine for this dinner tonight, rather than ringing down. The pleasure of books still placed where he had left them, and a lounge by the French windows that looked out to a view that was now familiar in its detail.

'Here I get to think,' Nico admitted, 'and there is a lot to think about.' He was hesitant, not used to wanting to speak about things, and he had shared this with no one. But somehow here with her and away from it all, Nico did relent and told her about his searching. 'I don't know where to look next.' He stabbed his fork into his dinner. 'How can I look for a birth record, when I don't even know my name?'

'You can't,' she said slowly, trying to hide the fear as to her family's part in this, trying to pretend that she didn't already know.

'After the wedding I walked around,' Nico said. 'I knew the streets…but I could not know them…' The bewildered frown on his face was completely out of place because even his forehead seemed to struggle to create the lines. Nico Eliades was a man who always knew the answers, always had things worked out. This, though, he still had not. 'Of course I can get nothing out of my parents. I have stopped asking for now. I figure if we are at least talking, maybe one day they will tell me.'

For the first time she saw it from his side. She'd seen it from her family's, had seen it from her own viewpoint—his wrath aimed at her when he found out the truth. But now she sat and saw it from his—the agony of knowing, and not having it confirmed.

'Nico…' She opened her mouth, but she did not know to broach it, how to say it.

'Leave it,' he said, because he was tired from it all. 'I'm going for a walk.'

He did. He walked the beach and back, and then he did it again, did not want to go to a bed that was empty and to the dream of what was waiting for him. He thought of her there in the house, and didn't like the comfort it brought, for he knew it could not last for long. He could hear the baby crying as he returned much later, saw her standing in the kitchen in a skimpy nightdress, waiting for a bottle to warm.

She turned and said nothing, guilt in her soul and trouble in her heart, because she could see the wretchedness inside him.

'I thought you…' He stopped then, because it should not merit conversation, it was no business of his how she fed her babe. 'Goodnight, then.'

She felt quite sure she was being dismissed. She headed to the bedroom and held tight to her baby, guilty tears coming as finally she put the teat of the bottle in Leo's mouth and he suckled eagerly. His dark eyes looking so lovingly up at her, not realising her guilt, unwitting of her failures.

Nico, she knew, would not be so easily fooled.

CHAPTER ELEVEN

AT FIRST her days had been spent dozing on the sofa—her energy seemed to have depleted along with her milk supply, and though Leo was far more content on the bottle, though there was far less for her to do, everything now seemed to exhaust her. Sometimes Connie would jump up, assuming Henry was summoning her, but gradually she learnt she didn't have to sleep with one ear open and with Nico working all day, slowly, slowly the fog started to lift. Connie took walks in the garden, or sat at the table doing a jigsaw Despina had found when clearing the house. Despina had given her other things, too. Late one afternoon when she'd been there a week or so, she handed Connie two bags. 'They are my niece's. I asked for you.'

Embarrassed, Connie was about to refuse, but she was touched and grateful, too, because it was awful facing Nico in the same round of baggy clothes. He'd suggested she go shopping, had told her he'd opened her an account for her in a couple of the boutiques, but the thought of walking into a place like that, let alone

Nico paying for it, had been more than enough reason to decline.

'Thank you.' As graciously as she could, she accepted the kind offer. Despina left the room and, after a moment, Constantine opened the bags, and realised that Despina's niece had style and a little daring, too.

There were shorts, skirts and tops that there was surely not a hope of getting into, but she did. Even if the tops were a little tight, there were cool billowing shirts that worked well with them. There was a vivid red bikini too, which she instantly stuffed back in the bag, but it felt wonderful to pull on different clothes, so wonderful that she took a long shower and shaved her legs, pulling on shorts for the first time since she'd left Xanos. A jade halter-neck top was a welcome splash of colour—and she told herself she was not dressing for him, but still, as she glanced at the clock, she couldn't help but smile at the time. The evenings were the best part of her day. Leo's nightime bath was a far more relaxed affair now and then she would dress him for bed and enjoy giving him his last drink. She settled him in his cot where he would roll straight on his side and start to suck his thumb, then she would wander in the garden for a while, taking in the fragrance of wild garlic that came in from the hill behind, watching the sun slide down, and thinking how lucky she felt to be there, how grateful she was for the reprieve.

But best of all in the evenings was the sound of the seaplane.

Because it brought him home.

She loved watching it touch down and then Nico step out. Sometimes the tide was in and the jetty submerged, but the plane would take him as close as possible and he would roll up his trousers and walk barefoot. She would have to keep looking away, to pretend not to be waiting, not to be watching, when he came in.

'How was your day?' she asked this evening.

'Impossible,' Nico told her, and then pulled out the phone and gave Charlotte the next day's orders. He'd spent the day in several town halls on the mainland, poring through records, and then, to cap things off, the extremely generous offer he had put in on the stretch of land beside his house had again been refused by the developer.

'I'll start dinner,' she offered.

'I'll get myself something later,' Nico said, because Despina always left him a feast of meals, but she ignored him and as she brushed past him Nico caught her fragrance. He saw how far she had come in these last days, and he wanted her on the couch weary and half-asleep, as she had been in London, because this version of Constantine was a one he was struggling to ignore. He went to place his laptop on the table, but the space was taken up by the outline of a huge jigsaw.

'Despina found it,' Connie apologised, 'though it doesn't have a picture to work from. It's handmade...'

He did not want to talk about jigsaws; he did not want to be standing here, wondering how Leo's day had been; he did not want to want the scent of home. He did not want her laying two plates on the bench. He selected a bottle of wine and opened it to breathe as she brought over the meal—a simple meal, of crisp salad with local olives and flakes of feta cheese warmed a little by slices of lamb tossed in oregano. There was a pita bread she had grilled, and though he did not want this, somehow they moved from the bench to the table. He sat there, doing the impossible jigsaw with one hand, idly eating from a fork with the other and it felt, for Nico, far too good to last.

'What time are the fireworks tonight?' She looked up from the jigsaw and he saw how much more readily she smiled these days.

'Fireworks?' Nico frowned.

'Well, it's morning in Australia,' she pointed out, because just as night fell here, Nico would head out to the garden with his phone. Just as Australia's working morning struck, so, too, did Nico, placing angry calls to the developer, furious at the lack of response to his questions and offers, clearly not used to being ignored or not getting his way. 'I want the jetty to be mine,' Nico said. 'It belongs to the next block of land. But I'll just have to go on wanting. He's knocked back my offer. I refuse to call again.'

'Till next time.' Connie grinned, and then it faded. 'I've got a difficult phone call to make, too. Not tonight,' she added, as they naturally moved from the table to the lounge. How much more comfortable she felt to sit beside him now. She looked out at the sea and thought for a quiet moment before speaking. 'But I have been putting it off.'

'To your parents?' Nico asked, but Connie shook her head.

Until she had sorted things with Nico, she could not stand to talk with them. She was injured, too, on behalf of Leo, the grandson they had made no effort to contact. 'I want to know how Stavros is.'

'Why?' Nico asked.

'Because,' Connie answered, 'I worry about him—I want to know how things are going...'

'After the way he treated you?' Nico shook his head. 'Why would you care for someone who hurt you?'

'It wasn't all his fault.'

'His part in it was, though,' Nico pointed out. 'He chose not to tell you the truth, he chose to deceive you.' He made a slicing gesture to his throat. 'Gone!'

'Just like that?' Connie challenged, and she wasn't defending Stavros, more she was defending herself. 'Sometimes things are more complicated—'

'Not really,' Nico interrupted. 'He lied to you, and in my book that means you don't have to worry about him any more.' He flicked his hand and said it again. 'Gone.'

She didn't like this conversation, didn't like learning the rules of relationships according to Nico, painfully aware that very soon it might be she who was gone, dismissed with a flick of his hand, for not telling what she knew.

'Anyway, let's not talk about it now,' Nico said, because tonight he could not accept just wanting. 'Let's just enjoy tonight.' And it wasn't what he said, more the way he said it that brought something back, that had her remember there was so much more to this man. He turned to face her on the sofa and smiled a smile she had seen before. With just one look he could melt her worries, with the merest lilt to his voice it was only them in the world. He leant over to pour her some wine, but she put her hand over the glass.

'Not for me, thanks.'

She couldn't quite work out what had happened, how the sofa had suddenly become the most dangerous place in the house.

'I'm going to bed. I'll just clear the bench.' She stood because Nico was stretching out on the sofa.

'Leave it,' Nico said. 'Despina will do it in the morning.'

She laughed, for the first time in…she honestly could not remember how long, possibly a year, but for the first time in ages Connie threw her head back and laughed. 'You were almost perfect there,' Connie explained. 'I thought you were going to clear it yourself.'

'Why would I?' The thought had never entered his head and she watched as he stretched out fully, and somehow she wanted to join him, to look out toward the darkened sea, to talk and, yes, perhaps laugh again, and maybe something more. 'Goodnight, Constantine.'

'Connie,' she corrected him, as she did so often, but Nico shook his head.

'Not to me.' She turned to walk toward the bedroom and his voice followed her. 'And by the way, I am.'

'Am what?' It came back to her then—a something that made her dare not turn around, and she stood holding her breath in the hallway, closing her eyes as she heard his response.

'Perfect.'

She walked to her bedroom, checked Leo and then climbed into bed, trying not to think about the *something* that had happened, but it was rippling through her body like a tide with no return. A mother, yes, she would always be a mother, but the wave was growing stronger, dousing her, as the woman she also was returned.

Nico Eliades was, to Connie, perfect.

It was she who was flawed.

CHAPTER TWELVE

SHE looked much the same to Nico when he poured real coffee from the pot and offered her one, but Connie, sitting on the sofa holding Leo, shook her head. She seemed unable to meet his eyes.

'Did you sleep well?' Nico asked.

'Wonderfully,' Connie said, taking great interest in her middle toenail, embarrassed by her own Nico-driven dreams. 'You?'

'Not so good.'

Nico was more concerned with the change in himself to notice any in Constantine, how he'd almost lost last night, at least where women were concerned, a very level head.

Last night, watching her eat, hearing her laugh, well, as she'd headed to bed, in an unguarded moment Nico knew he had flirted. It came as second nature to him, he consoled himself, with any beautiful woman…but there must be none of that, Nico firmly decided as the strained conversation went on. They hadn't sorted out the consequences of their first night together yet. It was not time think about moving on to their next.

'Did Leo's crying wake you?'

'A bit.'

It had.

It had been hell getting to sleep, sensing her in the next room and, like a punishment for the depravity of his own thoughts, every time he finally drifted off to sleep, the baby would wake him, and he would hear the murmur of her voice. He tried not to picture what she was wearing, if anything, tried not to go in there as he heard her settle the babe, tried to ignore the creak of her bed as she climbed back in it.

He had not considered at first that it might be a problem—his mind had been focussed on other things, the news he might have a son, the appalling conditions she was living in, but now they were away from all that, now that she was here in his house, in the next bedroom, suddenly he was remembering all too often, the bliss of their one night.

'I'm going to work.'

'Oh.' She tried to stifle the disappointment in her voice at his abruptness. He didn't look dressed for work—he hadn't shaved, he was wearing black jeans and a T-shirt and looked, Connie had thought, rather more casual than usual. There was nothing casual about her thoughts, though. He was sulky and dark and brooding and how she would kill for that smile, or more, for a kiss of those sullen lips.

'When will you be back?' And she could have bitten

her tongue off, because it sounded as if she was inter-ested, as if it mattered when he returned.

'Not sure.'

He did not answer to anyone, did not account for his movements—he had built his life around freedom. As he saw the seaplane land by the jetty to collect him he drained his coffee and stood to go then let out a mild curse.

'What?'

'I forgot.'

His mind hadn't particularly been on washing that morning in the shower and he raced in and grabbed the deodorant. He forgot again that life was different when she was near.

He walked out and lifted his shirt to spray the de-odorant, a simple movement that millions did each day, but he forgot how aware he was of her and now how aware she was of him. There was the strangest charge to the air as he exposed his stomach, just the flick of her eyes downwards to the olive skin and the black snake of hair, and because he had sprayed one side he had to spray the other, had to pretend he wasn't hard, had to pretend she had not seen.

Had to walk out without tasting her.

It was a relief that he was gone. The room came back into focus and it looked the same as it had before. There was the kitchen and the coffee pot, too, and there was Leo still in her arms, but how nearly he hadn't been.

How badly she had wanted to put him in his crib and

return to the room, to follow on with whatever had been about to take place.

'So, shoot me.' She smiled to Leo, who gave her a gummy one back. 'I fancy your father—it's hardly the crime of the century.' She heard the door open, jumped as she turned around, and standing there was Nico, and she knew he couldn't have heard her, was positive he hadn't, but she blushed to her roots any way.

'Actually…' He did not look at her as he walked to his bedroom, pulled out his case and started to pack some things. 'Something came up.' He had decided it at the stone arch, had made his decision and had turned around. 'I'm going to be away for a few days. There are things I need to attend to on the mainland.'

He did not wait for her response, did not look or say goodbye to Leo. Instead, he walked out of the door, and headed to the jetty, and she would see, because he was quite sure that she was watching, that not once did he turn around—for he dared not to love them.

CHAPTER THIRTEEN

IT WAS a week of thinking, of lying by the pool and trying to come to a decision as to how she could tell him,
and how that moment might present. Every evening she
sat doing the jigsaw, her eyes scanning the horizon for
a glimpse of his seaplane, but Nico didn't come home
and now Leo was sleeping through, the nights were so
long, and she wished, perhaps more than she should,
that he would call now and then.

And though he didn't call, though certainly she
missed him, it was also a week of healing, too.

With no Nico around, she was brave enough to pull
on the red bikini and the sun felt familiar on her body
as she walked outside. The same sun that lit the globe,
except here in Xanos it shone as it should. The shadows
fell as they always had as she walked across the stone
and the sultry, humid scent it delivered to the garden
as it warmed it was one she had grown up with. The
ocean, too, sounded as it should when she closed her
eyes and lay there. She enjoyed chatting with Despina,
who desperately missed her niece; and even though they

spoke on the phone weekly, it wasn't the same, Despina said, as having her there.

'She'll be back,' Connie offered, but saw the worry lines in Despina's kind face deepen.

'To what?' She gestured to the opulent view, the hotel and the huge houses. 'The locals cannot afford to live here—there will be nothing for her to come to soon. And once the houses are torn down...' she gave a worried shrug '...I won't be here, either.'

'Torn down?'

'That is what Nico said when he hired us. He is having plans drawn up.' She gave a weary smile. 'For now we have a job and somewhere to live. Who knows? When it is done, maybe he will keep us on, though we like our little house.' She smiled properly now when she looked down at Leo, who was lying on a rug in the shade, and then she stood. 'I'd better get on.'

Bloated when she'd arrived from poor diet and exhaustion, now that Connie slept at night and ate the fruits of Xanos, her body rewarded her with its return. The sun's rays were not just warming, but shining light on past hurts, till she could see more clearly and, though she would never let herself be treated like that again, she could understand now why Stavros had behaved as he had.

And there was a call to be made.

To the man who would have been her husband. After, she wept in relief that the conversation had been amicable, pleasant even—she had not realised till then that, despite the way he had treated her, she had been scared for him, could see that he had been as trapped as her. But Stavros was happy now, grateful for what had happened even, for he was on the mainland, living the life he had been born to.

A small plane on the horizon had Connie's heart leap. As it landed by the jetty, she considered putting on her blouse to cover herself, but she needn't worry as the passenger that stepped out certainly wasn't Nico.

Blond, stunning, in a black suit and killer stilettos, a mere wisp of a thing tottered along the jetty, pausing every now and then to take photos of the house and then of the ocean. The woman edged her way nearer, till her blonde head disappeared from view and, a moment or two later, Connie heard her clipping in her high heels up the garden.

'Hi, I'm Charlotte.' Of course she was, Connie thought with a sinking heart. 'Nico asked me to get some photos of the hill and the jetty. Gosh...' she looked down at Leo '...he's gorgeous.'

'Thank you.'

'Aren't they lovely when they're that small and can't answer back at you? It's a shame it doesn't last.'

'Do you have children?' Connie asked, then wished she hadn't bothered. That toned, flat stomach and those tiny pert breasts, and the absolutely immaculate hair and make-up dictated the answer.

'God, no.' Charlotte let out a laugh. 'Unless you count Nico—it's like running around after an angry toddler at the moment. He's hell bent on getting this next bit of land.'

So he can get busy tearing things down, Connie thought sadly.

'How is he?' Charlotte suddenly asked, and, when Connie frowned, she clarified, 'The baby—is he settling in?'

'He's fine.' She didn't like sitting here, fat in her red bikini and shiny with oil, as this gorgeous thing stood ice cool in the late afternoon sun. 'Look, can I get you a drink or anything?'

'No thanks.' She gave a cheery smile. 'There's plenty on the plane. Nice to meet you.' She gave a small wave and then clipped off, leaving Connie feeling… She tried to pin it down. Angry wasn't the word, more…stupid. Stupid to even think that he could ever really want her. Nico wanted freedom, Connie wanted him all. Charlotte was so much more suitable for him, so much more like him.

No wonder he'd lasted barely a week here with her. No doubt he'd fled straight to Charlotte the moment the refugees had been housed. Despina came and took Leo inside, and Connie was still bristling, hating that she wondered when she would see Nico again. She tried hard not to think of him and instead let the sea lull her and the soft sounds of early evening lull her. She could hear Charlotte's seaplane taking off and its hum in the distance, and closed her eyes, but all she could think of was him.

'Constantine.' She jumped as she opened her eyes, flat on her back and wearing so little was so not how she wanted to be seen by him. It had never entered her head that he was here.

'How come...?' She wanted to cover herself, but just lay there, looked up at him and couldn't read the expression on his face. 'Charlotte didn't mention you were on your way.'

Charlotte hadn't known till a couple of moments ago, Nico thought. She'd stepped back on the plane, where he had been waiting, and relayed what he had asked her to check on. 'He's fine,' Charlotte had said, but it simply hadn't been enough to just hear it. 'She seems fine' hadn't been enough, either. He'd sat on the air-conditioned plane, as Charlotte had taken pictures that weren't even needed, determined not to go out, except, seeing his home, knowing they were in it, there had been a pull stronger than gravity that had dragged him here. He was resisting it still, even as he stood looking down at her. Never had she looked more beautiful. It was not about weight, or how the bikini set his mind in dangerous directions, but a new confidence in her, the painted nails, the smooth, oiled skin and the luxury of her hair let loose. It looked like a curtain over the lounger and he did not understand why her confidence rattled him so.

'I'm going inside.' He walked in and took a long drink of water, resisted going to her bedroom, for he did not want to get involved with the baby and, yes, there was much on his mind.

Work had been busy this week, yet it hadn't fully occupied him. There had been more fruitless searches in an attempt to sort out the mystery of his life and he had considered staying in Athens, to try and free his head from Constantine and her baby. He had intended to grab freedom while he'd had it, yet there had been a pull to go home and, no matter how he had fought it, no matter how much he had known that they were okay, there had been a need to see them for himself.

He glanced towards the garden and then he saw her climbing off the lounger, and something close to fear clutched him, because the woman who stretched and walked luxuriously towards the house, unaware of male eyes on her, was the woman he had known one day soon she would become.

Constantine had emerged from herself, which meant, as he had promised, soon he must confront her, must find out the truth about Leo. And then what?

They would leave.

Leave because they had to, because this wasn't his life, this wasn't what he wanted, wasn't something he could keep.

'What did you get up to this week?' he asked as she walked into the kitchen.

'Slept, sunbaked...' There was a tinge of guilt in her admission. 'I'm going to do some gardening next week...'

'You're not here to garden.'

'But I'd enjoy it.'

'No,' Nico said. 'I did not ask what you did and expect a long list to justify your time—I was making conversation. I am glad that you are resting, it is good to see you looking better.' So very much better, so much, in fact, that it might be prudent if she went and changed, because the flimsy shirt she had put on over her bikini left little to a suddenly active imagination.

'I rang Stavros.' He raised his eyes just a little, searched her face for evidence of upset, but she was still calm.

'How was he?'

'Well.' She smiled. 'And he is happy.' Nico gave a shrug—he didn't like Stavros and neither did he like what he had put Constantine through. 'He has been through some difficult times.'

'So?' Nico asked. 'That does not mean you forgive.'

'Well, I can. His difficult times have lasted a lot longer than mine—he's been struggling with this for years. I can see now why he was angry, perhaps mean to me at times...' Nico looked less than convinced, so she changed the topic to something far lighter, something that still made her smile even now. 'Actually, I do have some news!' The sun was coming through the window behind, but it wasn't as bright as her smile, and it was a Constantine he had never seen, even on their one night together. There was a lightness to her, a calmness, and it reached him, had him smiling back in return. 'We don't need a box.'

'Sorry?'

'This is your box.' He had no idea what she talking about. All he could see as she walked over to the table were long brown legs, all he could think of as he walked over to where she stood was the scent of her close up—a feminine scent, a summer scent of oil and woman. She waved at the French windows and he had to force himself to turn his head towards them rather than towards her mouth. 'It's the view from here.'

She was right. He looked at the jigsaw and she had been busy. There was the frame of the windows and a dash of red geranium. There was the azure of the pool, the white of the balcony and the red of the flowers. He looked at the jumble of loose pieces, her fingers selecting one and slotting it in as she spoke.

'Paulo was trimming the bush,' Constantine explained, 'and I could see it. Someone has painted the view and then made it into a jigsaw.'

'Shame,' Nico said. 'It would surely be better hung on the wall.'

'I think it's fun,' Constantine said, and that admission surprised even her, for that word hadn't been in her vocabulary for a very long time. 'Oh!' She saw another piece, and her hand moved and collected it. 'It's a baby,' she said, slotting it into its place. He did not care for jigsaws but he was starting to care more for her. He looked at the concentration on her face, the shimmer of her skin, and his next question came from a place he did not know, a place he should not go, but it was a place within that wanted to know.

'How is Leo?'

'Wonderful!' Deliberately she didn't look up, tried not to seem as if she'd noticed, but her heart tripped faster, for it was the first time he had asked about his baby. Another piece of jigsaw caught her eye and, as nonchalantly as she could, she told him some more. 'Bathed and fed and fast asleep. I took him in the pool for a little while. Despina said it was too soon, but he laughed and loved it…'

He wished he had seen it.

'Here's another one.' He picked up another piece of the puzzle and slotted it in. 'Another baby, they must be twins.' He looked at where she stood, saw her rapid blink and her face redden, and he mistook the reason. He thought she must be suddenly aware of how little she had on, or knew perhaps how much he wanted her.

And he didn't want to want her.

'I'm going to get changed.' His voice was gruffer than intended and Constantine glanced up and frowned.

'Are you okay?'

'Fine.'

He was far from fine.

Nico was uncomfortable, unsettled, because that walk up the beach, to the stairs, the conversation, for the first time he had felt as if he was coming home— that feeling he had got as he had seen the view of his house had been, Nico now realised, relief.

But it did not soothe him now.

There could be no getting used to it.

He heard a murmur from her room as he walked past, a small wail of distress, and he ignored it. Constantine would get him if he awoke, would soothe him if he cried.

And then it came again and Nico stopped in the hallway.

He closed his eyes and tried to force himself to walk away, yet his feet moved toward her room, to the scent of her, layered with another scent, that sweet, milky, baby scent that was becoming familiar. He had never really looked at the infant, had deliberately tried to separate himself from him.

Because if he was his, what then?

And if he wasn't?

He moved towards the crib and peered in, with no intention of doing anything, for Nico had never so much as held a baby. But on sight instinctively he knew what was wrong. Leo had lost his thumb. His little hand was caught in the cotton and with heart racing Nico took the baby's hand and moved it back to his mouth. He smiled at Leo's relief as he popped his thumb in. His finger pushed up his nose to a snub, his eyelashes so long that they met the curve of his cheek, and Nico's heart stilled as Leo opened his eyes to his saviour. Huge black eyes stared at Nico, and a smile flitted across the baby's face. Then, soothed by what he saw, Leo closed his eyes again.

Nico's heart did beat again but with something that felt like fear, for he recognised him.

Of course he did, Nico told himself, for he was his.

He walked to the bathroom, his breathing hard as if he had been running, sweat beading on his forehead. He felt ill, dizzy, that perhaps he, all six feet two of him, might fall to the floor in a faint.

'Ridiculous.'

He moved to the sink, ran the taps hard and splashed water on his grey face.

So, the child was his—it could hardly come as a shock. He looked in the mirror to scold himself, to tell himself to pull himself together, but the eyes that looked back, the reflection that stared, only confused him more.

He put his hand to the mirror, and his reflection did the same, which must mean it was him.

He wanted them gone.

He did not love.

And it was love Constantine wanted, not passion or romance or just the house and land and the trappings—it was everything she wanted, and love was the one thing he could not give. This would not last. He lived in the fast lane, he liked his freedom. How soon would he be bored, how soon would she leave?

She *would* leave. Nico intrinsically knew that, and quite simply he wanted it done. Wanted it over.

He would show her his life, show her firsthand the world he inhabited; he would push her away by her own choice.

Prove how incompatible they were.

She was slicing salad in the kitchen, so confident in her own skin now that she had not gone and dressed. He could see her breasts moving as she sliced, see her brown, sun-kissed stomach, and he could not do this for another night.

He could not let her think this was how he lived. He would show her instead just how impossible they were, push her out of her comfort zone as much as she pushed him out of his.

'I'm bored eating in.' He saw her eyes jerk up. 'We should go out.' Because that was what he did—he ate out, not home-made salads and jigsaws afterwards, not the walk on the beach she might suggest later tonight.

'Sure.' She hesitated for a moment, just surprised, that was all. 'I'll get Leo.'

'Just us.'

She was about to give a smart retort for his abruptness, but conceded she had perhaps misinterpreted his words, and anyway the prospect of a night out was tempting.

'I'll see if Despina can babysit.'

When Connie walked over to her house and asked her, Despina said she would be delighted to, of course. Not that Nico seemed particularly pleased by the news when she returned. 'I've rung Charlotte and she's arranged a table and driver—we leave in half an hour.'

'Why would we need a driver when you've got a car?' Connie asked, for there there was a sports car in the garage that she'd never seen him take out.

'I might want a drink.'

'Then it's a beautiful evening to walk.'

'You want to walk to Ravels?' He looked at where she stood in just a bikini and shirt, and threw her his impossible order, and made sure she understood. 'It's quite a distance and I assume you'll be wearing heels—it's very smart.'

He wasn't, Constantine realised, trying to impress her with his choice of venue.

Quite the opposite. Perhaps he was hoping she would change her mind, find an excuse or reason not to go.

Well, she wouldn't give him the satisfaction. Instead, she smiled to him.

'Then I'd better get ready.'

Why she was putting herself through this? Connie wasn't sure, except she would not be intimidated by Nico.

From the wrong side of Xanos she may be, and certainly wasn't the sleek and groomed beauties he was used to dining with, but she refused to sit at home feeling not good enough.

She showered quickly and, realising there was no time to dry her hair as she usually would, she hung her head down and blasted it with a hairdryer. She would decide what to do with it later. She fled to her bedroom, wondering what on earth she should wear, because nothing Despina had brought her would be okay for the restaurant, and she'd worn everything so many times anyway.

It was hopeless. All her own clothes had been stretched out of shape by her pregnancy, except...

Connie pulled her suitcase from under her bed. There, still in the tissue paper, was the dress she should have worn as she was waved off for her honeymoon. Instead, that night had been spent telling Stavros and then her parents that a token wife she could not be.

Unwrapping the tissue paper, all Constantine could

really remember of the dress was that it was purple, but as the paper parted she corrected herself. It was a very deep violet and made of the softest virgin cashmere and silk. It had cost a lot more than she had told her parents it had when she had come back from a day shopping with friends in Athens.

Her once guilty purchase was now her saviour, for her spending had been reckless that day, and Constantine blinked as she saw the forgotten underwear she had purchased. After months of being practical, it felt like heaven to pull on the delicate lace panties, and the bliss of a new bra gave Connie a boost in more ways than one.

Please fit.

She pulled the dress over her head and wriggled the soft fabric over curves that hadn't been there the last time she had tried it on. As it fell over her hips she was almost scared to open her eyes at her own reflection, quite sure it would look terrible now, but as she looked into the mirror, it looked far from terrible. It looked so much better than she recalled—her bust filled out the dress. The bra made her cleavage look endless, and the wrap of the dress hid any last baby bulge.

It was a dress called confidence, and she felt hers return, felt something else, too, a shiver of excitement, an anticipation as to his response.

If he was expecting her to emerge from the bedroom to tell him she had changed her mind, then Nico was in for a shock.

For the first time since that terrible row with her parents, since she had found out she was pregnant and the desperate survival mode she had been plunged into, she opened her make-up bag, took out her hair tongs and plugged them in and then worked on her face. She applied some mineral foundation and rouge, and coaxed a rather dry mascara wand to please give her one last bat of her lashes, and it did. She ran serum through her thick dark hair and, instead of twisting it and putting it up, or tying it back as she always did, she accentuated the curls by twirling them into ringlets. All she needed now was lipstick, her lips smiling as they were reacquainted with the soft, waxy feel. She stepped into heels that had never been worn, and felt as if she was stepping into herself.

'Despina is here to watch Leo.' She heard Nico's sharp summons and looked at her reflection. A devilish smile appeared on her lips.

'Just coming.'

God, but she'd have killed for some perfume, to waft out of her room in a sultry haze, or for a heavy necklace to accentuate her cleavage, but her only accessory was her smile.

It was a smile that greeted Despina and completely ignored Nico as she stepped into the lounge.

'Beautiful.' The old lady said everything Nico did not. He just stood there, completely rigid.

'You know where everything is,' Connie chatted, and then suddenly she remembered. 'Your niece is ringing you tonight.'

'Don't worry.' Despina dismissed it as if it didn't

matter, but Connie knew that it did. Despina had been talking today about how excited she was to speak with her niece, how much she looked forward to their weekly chat. 'Do you want to look after him in your house?' She knew how Despina adored Leo, how much care she would take, and how the elderly couple would love to have him in their own surroundings. They deserved their evening together after all.

'Are you sure?' Despina checked. Connie knew it was the right thing to do, but her stomach tightened into a knot when Despina suggested that Paulo bring over the crib and they keep him for the night. 'Then you don't have to worry about what time you come back.'

It made sense, it made perfect sense, rather than disturbing them at midnight, but as she nodded, as Paulo came over and she packed a bag of supplies, as she kissed her son goodnight and said goodbye to him at the door, the knot in her stomach was for different reason.

They were alone for the first time.

Somehow with Leo there, she felt safer. Not safer in the physical sense, but he gave her a reason, a topic, a diversion. Connie held her breath as she watched the trio go out of sight—Leo gave her an excuse to be here. Now it was just them.

Her smile didn't come so readily now but she forced one and turned around.

'I just saw the car.' Still Nico said nothing. 'I'll get my purse.'

'Why would you need a purse?' Nico said. 'I am taking you out.'

'Because,' Connie said, and walked past him. And, yes, her purse was a little faded and not particularly a match for her dress, but she would not leave without it. What would Nico know about the security it afforded, to know that she could leave anywhere at any time? That even through the most desperate of times, there was enough money to get a taxi for her and her child should she need it, though perhaps not enough to pick up the bill in this restaurant should Nico walk out, which, Connie realised, was a distinct possibility in his present mood.

'Anyway…' His next words bought her racing mind to calm decision. 'I doubt you could afford to go halves.'

And she had promised she would not do this.

She could remember all too well the long, painful dinners with Stavros, the family affairs where she had gone home afterwards and to bed in tears. For no matter how she had tried to please him, it had never been enough. She remembered how badly Stavros had spoken to her at times, and she had sworn never again.

'I've changed my mind,' she said, what he had been expecting all along, but it was for very different reasons. 'I don't think I want to go.'

'I thought you might change your mind.' Nico said tartly. 'Well, I need to get out. I've had enough of sitting in—'

'So have I,' Connie interrupted. 'And I was looking forward to a night out with you, but I really don't need to be reminded that I'm a charity case, and neither do I want to sit opposite someone who can't be bothered to speak to me or doesn't even tell me that I look nice.'

'You need my opinion?'

'I need manners!' Connie said. 'It shouldn't matter what I'm wearing.' She wasn't about to explain herself to him. 'I'm really not up to gauging your mood.' She walked past him to the door. 'I'll tell the driver you're coming.'

'Where are you going?'

'For a walk,' Connie said. 'I might go to and have dinner at the taverna.'

'Alone?'

'Of course.' She frowned. 'I haven't had a night off since Leo was born. I intend to enjoy every moment of it—and I'm wasting several of them now.'

Her response was nothing like he had expected.

Nothing like he was used to.

She would, Nico knew then, she absolutely would go out without him.

Tonight was about pushing her away, showing her the impossibility of it—except far from pushing her away, instead his hand reached out and caught her wrist and pulled her towards him.

'You can't go alone.'

'Why not?' she challenged. 'What, you think I need you to go out with? That I need an escort? I'm very happy with my own company. I know *she* won't sulk, I know *she'll* enjoy the evening.'

'You look…' He hesitated, because she looked far more than the word she had demanded. 'Nice.'

'I know,' Connie answered. 'Now, if you'll let go of my wrist, I've got a date with me.'

'You look beautiful.'

'You don't get it, do you? I'm not talking about compliments or the lack of them. I just refuse to sit and drag conversation out of you, to be grateful to you for taking me to a stunning place. You've been vile since you came home—and I don't want your company.'

'I'm sorry.' It was possibly the first time he had ever said it and certainly to a woman. Normally it was they who were sorry, begging for a second chance, saying that they would change, if only he wouldn't end things. 'I'm sorry if I have been, as you say, vile. I didn't intend…' He could hardly tell her that he had never expected her to say yes and had certainly never expected the woman that had emerged from the bedroom. And more importantly, he had never intended this night to prove how much he wanted her, to confirm what his body already knew.

She felt the charge run through his fingers to her wrist like electricity, watched the surly man who'd come home slip into tempting lover as he pulled her in, heard the taut voice slip into caressing as the skilled seducer emerged. And she fought it, so hard she fought it. His lips apologised, this time to her mouth, and, God, it was bliss to be back there. To the mouth she'd missed for a year, to hands that roamed her body as if abstinence had been hell. His tongue prised her lips open before her mind was really aware of it. On contact they ignited, two mouths became one. He turned her so her back was to the wall and he kissed her harder.

Their one night had been a long lesson, a more tender guide to a place that was waiting. This was a run and he was chasing, his hands moving to the tie of her dress. He moaned into her mouth as he felt purple lace.

From so little experience, she thought it would take ages, that tenderness was required, but with hungry hands searching, with Nico's passion contagious, she was a breath away from joining him, from tearing at his clothes, just to get them to that place.

And then she remembered the doctor's words, which she had barely even registered at the time, because sex had seemed a million light years off. Given her success with the Pill, he had put in an IUD, but he had told her the first time afterwards to take things slowly, that her partner must be gentle.

As good as this was, gentle it was not.

What would Nico know about these things? How could he possibly understand the sudden nervousness and that had her quickly pull away?

'The driver's here.' She turned her face from his hungry kisses and quickly tied up her dress.

'He can wait,' Nico said.

'Well, I can't.' Connie almost ran to the bathroom to fix her face, calling over her shoulder as she went, 'I'm starving.'

So fierce was his want, as she sat in the car Connie was nervous, she could feel the charge between them, felt like she was keeping a tiger at bay with a paltry stick. She knew sex was on the menu tonight, but how could she explain her nerves at making love after the baby—not at the changes to her body but the anticipation of pain?

As the car pulled up, Nico turned to her and she knew exactly what he was suggesting. 'We could get them to deliver.'

'I thought you were bored, eating in.'

His hand was hot and dry as it closed around hers, his thumb pressing into her palm as they walked in. And Connie could not have cared less about the other guests. Her mind was only on him, on tonight, on the thought of this beautiful man unleashed. And in a place where heads usually refused to turn because it meant someone was more interesting, when the two of them entered and were led through the restaurant to a balcony table, heads did turn, such was their energy, such was the pulse that throbbed between them.

She had always known that he was beautiful, but even here he stood out—and curious eyes looked at them, trying to place him, for certainly he was someone.

He ordered champagne.

'Which is what you were drinking when I found you.' And it was a curious choice of words, Connie thought, but that was exactly as it had been. That night, not only had Nico found her but she had started to find herself. 'But I'll treat you to a glass this time!'

She loved his humour, loved it that when she smiled

at his words, then so, too, did he. Private memories wrapped around them at a small table and he was, for once, so unguarded, so delicious that when the waiter came over, she wanted to ask if rope was on the menu: she needed tethering to the chair, just so she wouldn't go over to him.

The champagne was delicious. Unlike that first night, today she tasted it. Connie liked the taste, the cool and the bubbles and, with Nico opposite, his eyes making love to her already, every sense was heightened. She could smell the fragrant herbs from the kitchen, hear the chatter and laughter surrounding them and feel the breeze from the ocean cooling her cheeks. She was aware of her own breasts as she leant forward, saw him swallow as he glimpsed violet lace—and tonight he would have her, of that she was deliciously, albeit, terrifyingly certain.

It was nice to be out.

So nice to not have one ear open for her baby, so nice to concentrate on the conversation, to be here with this beautiful man, except it was too nice sometimes, for as they spoke, as they shared a little more of themselves with each other she was reminded, as if she could ever forget it, of the terrible day that was surely to come.

'I met with a detective today,' Nico said, and her cutlery hesitated over her food, and she had to remind herself to cut it, had to speak as though dread were not clutching her heart.

'Has he found anything out?'

'Nothing.' Nico let out a hiss of frustration. 'Every

hospital, the children's home, adoption agencies…there was no adoption, he says. Or rather, no legal one. This weekend I am going to speak to my parents. I want answers.'

'Will they help?' Connie asked, and her heart was truly torn between protecting her family or telling him.

'Probably not.'

'You're not even sure that you are adopted.' She burnt with guilt as she tried to divert him.

'I'm sure.' Black eyes met hers. 'I sat on that ferry on the way to the wedding and I could her a baby screaming… I was on that ferry…' It was too hard to explain it.

'Will knowing change anything?' He did not answer. It was, Connie decided, the most stupid question. He had a right to know his history, a right to know his past. It was her family's part in it that had prevented her from revealing the truth. If it weren't for that she would be helping him, supporting him, instead of sitting here lying and praying that somehow he might forgive her when he found out, might not destroy the family that, despite it all, she loved. 'There might have been reasons…'

'Then I have a right know them,' Nico said darkly, because every night he dreaded sleep, every time he looked in the mirror he felt as if were going mental. Every time his parents denied it, they lied just a little bit more and he needed to know and then he needed revenge.

'Where would you go?' She glanced up from her dinner, confused by his question. 'If you could not have coped with Leo?' Nico asked. 'If you wanted him adopted.'

'I've never given it a thought.' She gave a shrug, felt her breathing grow shallow.

'Please, Constantine, think for me.'

'Maybe the church…'

'Or, what if you wanted a baby?' Nico pushed, and she felt as if fingers were moving around her throat and slowly choking her.

'To the church,' she said again.

'If it had been the church it would be documented. Where would you go…?' He was talking more to himself than to her, but every word shot through her. He would speak to the doctors, Nico told her, and to the doulas… He would hire another detective. With every thought he inched closer to the unpalatable truth and it wasn't a question of diverting him. Her heart wanted him to know.

And she would not wait for him to find out. Connie knew what was right now, it must be she that told him.

'You'll find out soon.' She slipped her hand to his and he took it and she meant every last word on her lips. Not now, not here, but this weekend she would choose the moment.

And he took her hand and he held it, and for the first time he thought that maybe she could be his.

That maybe this could work, that his heart might be one worth sharing.

CHAPTER FOURTEEN

LOVE entered his heart and this time he did not reject it, did not consider it impossible, for how could he, now that she was here?

'I want you.' He looked at her and he neither extended his words nor qualified them, but it made her heart soar to see love in his eyes, to feel the want shared between them.

They stripped prawns with their fingers, fingers that met in the bowl on the table and entwined for a moment in the tepid water. She removed her hand, because surely it was mad to sit holding hands in water, but as he had pressed the slice of lemon between thumb and finger she had had to swallow a breath, for it felt as if low, low in her stomach and down to her thighs, he was stroking.

The food *was* divine.

So much she noticed. As she tasted the produce of her island Connie savoured each mouthful, licked the oil from her lips and wished it was him.

'No dessert menu.' He made the decision for them.

He could not sit there one moment, could not watch her eat something sticky and sweet, could not watch that tongue lick those lips for even a second longer if it wasn't on him, and, no, they didn't want coffee, either.

Thank God he had an account there, so when to not be touching became unbearable, he didn't have to worry about the bill, could simply take her by the hand and lead her out.

'I'm trying not to break into a run,' he said low into her ear as they walked through the restaurant.

He did not kiss her in the car—could not stand to start and have to stop again.

They walked through the arch. The night was warm and the thin wool of her dress felt oppressive now as she climbed the steps. They were both nervous and excited about what lay ahead. She heard the driver move off. Finally it was just them and because he had waited all night, he could wait no more, could not make it to the door without tasting what he had desired. But when he moved to kiss her, when they were alone, her kisses were not as expected. So he kissed her harder, undid the wrap of her dress, as he had wanted to before, and peeled it open and down her shoulders. Then stared at the breasts that had entranced him all night. He lowered his head to them as he slid the dress down her arms.

She felt ridiculous, there by the pool in her pants and bra, but the night air was cool on her bare skin and slowly, with his tender attention, she relaxed just a little. His mouth on her breasts was sublime, and she knew that now she could confide, because Nico was more than a lover, he was her heart.

'I'm scared it will hurt.' She felt the flutter of his lashes against her breast and knew he had closed his eyes. His mouth stilled and he lifted his head to hers.

He could have kicked himself, thought of how he had been before, understood now why she had halted him, and he said something he meant.

'I'd never hurt you,' Nico said, and he hesitated, for, for a second there, he wasn't just talking about sex. He never made promises like that, never said things to which he would not adhere, but truly he meant it now.

'Let's cool off.' He gestured to the pool and she laughed as he started to take off his suit.

'We can't!'

'Why not?'

'Because…' She was shivering with both reluctance and temptation. Reluctance, because it seemed wrong somehow; tempted, because Nico, so uninhibited, was already undressed, and she was gifted again with the sight of his body. Her eyes flicked down to what awaited. He beckoned her to the water.

'No one can see or hear us.' He was right. Despina's house was tucked well away, and the pool was shaded by a huge fig tree. There was nothing to stop her from going in. In fact, Nico was already in. Looking up, she felt his adoring scrutiny as she took off her shoes. She stood and looked down at him as she unhooked her bra and took it off, and she smiled unseen, for he was certainly not looking at her face. And he closed his eyes, just for a second as she slid down her pants, then opened them again to issue an order.

'Stay there.' He asked her to stay just to see her, to look just once more at all that he had missed for a year. His eyes told her, told her as they slowly took her in, that this was all he had been thinking of for a very long time now.

And then he held out his hand to her and the water was bliss to slip into, his wet arms better still.

His kiss was slow, measured and tender, but still nerves made her shiver because she could feel every inch of him against her stomach, but there was some relief, for now he was in no rush.

'Let me wash you.'

He made her smile, but *wash* her tenderly he did. His hands moved over her, washed her as if they contained soap. He washed her arms and then her fingers and then her back and then her breasts and then he rinsed her, scooped the water over. Then the imaginary soap washed her face and ears with both his mouth and fingers, and so gentle was he, so slow and caressing, that she almost forgot to be scared.

Not even when his hands moved beneath the water, when he *washed* her most intimate place. When his fingers delicately moved in each crevice, all she could do was lean on his shoulder and nibble and moan against his saltwater skin.

She was as slippery, deep inside, as if he *had* used soap, Nico could feel it. Now she was ready, and so, absolutely, was he.

She wrapped her legs around him, felt the cold stone against her back. He lowered her down to him and there was no stab like before, just a slow, accepting stretch. The water was calm and still, despite the fire beneath the surface, as she let him take her, as she trusted herself to his skill. He supported her body with his hands, the water barely moving; he was so slow and tender, and then he moved her some more, till she wanted more, till her legs wrapped tighter around him and Connie moved to her own rhythm as he still supported her.

On the surface they were just kissing, kissing mouth, face and shoulders, but they were intimately united beneath, locked in each other, till she could not kiss and just rested her head to the side of his. And was it the words he uttered or the throb of him that made her feel giddy? A heat spread out from a deep centre and coherence was abandoned, just a strangled laugh to dismiss his apology as his hands pushed her hips harder down, for her own orgasm rushed in to meet his. It was so intense and so deep that it shot to her spine, to her throat and seized at her brain, halting words, for which she was thankful, because she almost told him she loved him. And in that moment, she was sure, he would have loved her right back, a declaration might have been made, without Nico knowing all the facts.

She felt like a liar as he helped her out of the pool. Her legs were shaky once on firmer ground, and she could not look at him so bent to get her clothes instead.

'Leave it.'

'I am not leaving this for Despina!' Because she

knew he was not talking about leaving it to the morning, but to see Nico pick up, when he never did, to see Nico look up as she watched and smiled, she felt like crying, because he wasn't almost perfect—he simply was.

'Constantine?' She heard the question in his voice as they headed back to the house, but she could not answer him. Instead, automatically, she headed to her bedroom to check on Leo and gave a small embarrassed laugh as he walked up behind her and she realised what she was doing.

'Sheer habit,' Connie said, but her laugh faded a little, because it did feel strange to be without Leo, strange to go to Nico's bed and know her baby was not in the house.

'You miss him?' Nico asked as she lay in the dark next to him.

'Yes,' Connie admitted. 'I mean, I've had the most wonderful night. It just feels a bit strange, not having him near.' There was the longest pause and then Nico asked a question.

'How could she?' Nico asked. 'How could she just give up her baby?'

'I'm sure she had her reasons.' Connie could feel her heart hammering in her chest. 'I don't think you should judge her without…' Unseen, she closed her eyes at the thought of all that was to come, of the pain she must soon inflict, and her voice wasn't quite as assured when next it came. 'Without knowing.'

She would tell him in the morning, before Despina

brought Leo back. She would give him the starting point from where to look, and maybe he wouldn't blame her, Connie tried to reassure herself. Maybe he might forgive her for not telling him sooner.

But even safe in his arms, it was hard to rest on a bed of so many maybes.

CHAPTER FIFTEEN

HE FORCED his eyes open before he jumped, his heart racing, unlike the slow dawn.

How he hated to dream, hated the fear that claimed him while unguarded. His dreams were now of babies, who were walking and talking, dreams of a hundred babies that looked like him.

He should let her sleep, Nico told himself. It was, after all, her first full night away from Leo, her first chance to sleep as long as her body dictated, though his body dictated otherwise. Nico did not like sex in the morning—it was too intimate for him, brought the reckless night into another day, made her think this closeness might continue.

This would.

Again he let himself glimpse the possibility—a future with Constantine as his wife and Leo his son, with a home and a garden of memories. His hands roamed her body and he could feel her soft and warm. What had made him think he might lose them? What, with her here, could possibly go wrong?

She lay there, feeling him awaken beside her.

Felt his hands softly probe her and she could not lie for her family, could not live with deceit for a second longer.

He was nudging behind her, his lips on the back of her neck, and she wanted him inside her, but she wanted to make love with the truth uniting them, not the terrible guilt of the lie she hadn't told.

'Nico…' She wriggled away from him. 'Can I tell you something?'

'Tell me here,' Nico said, pulling her towards him, but she rolled on her back.

'Nico, please…it's important.'

It *was* important.

He wanted to hear that Leo was his son; he wanted to know that she loved him.

Wanted to be inside her when she told him about the family they were.

'Tell me.' He rolled on top of her, he kissed her face, he welcomed the news, for he had been wrong. You did not lose, love did not leave. She felt his thigh part her legs, felt the claim of his kiss, and she turned her face away.

'Nico, please…' He slipped inside as if he belonged there. Her body was ready for him but her mind was not, for she had to tell him. 'I know who arranged your adoption.'

She waited for him to stop, for him to die inside her, for him to haul himself off, but there was just a pause, not even a second, an energy that changed.

He looked down at the woman who would have made him a father, who he would have loved for the rest of his life, and she held the answers he had been seeking, just not the ones for which he had hoped.

She knew it was over even as he thrust inside her, she knew from this they could not survive—that he would never hold her again, that she would never feel him again—and she wanted this time, shared in his anger, for she, too, lost.

He pinned her with his body, and she wanted the weight because she wanted to feel him. She wanted the power and the energy and anger of this man, and the anaesthetic of being conjoined.

She tightened around him and tried to halt her own orgasm, tried to calm the flare, tried for it not to be over, for then she would have to face him.

But Nico wanted otherwise.

He wanted it over, he wanted release; he felt her body tame when he wanted it wild, and he worked faster for it, harder for it, till her body could hold back no more and she cried as he pulsed inside her, because she knew now she must face him.

'You know?'

He looked down at her. He was still inside her and there was no escape from his eyes.

'How long?' He did not ask about his past, his questions were solely as to her part in this. 'How long have known?'

'I found out last year.' She wanted to be back in his arms, but he rolled from her, breathless, ominously calm. He sat up in the bed, shot out an incredulous, mirthless laugh and then his face turned to hers and she saw him look now at the witch who had deceived him, for the love had gone from his eyes.

'And you let me keep looking? You've seen me searching…' His mouth was in the shape of a smile, but she made no mistake that he was taking it well. She could see the muscles on his shoulders tighten, fury descended as he took it all in.

'I didn't know how to tell you.'

'Well, *darling,* you'd better find the way now.' It was no endearment. The word curled with disdain as he voiced it.

'I found your birth certificate, the real one…' There was no easier way to say it. 'In my father's office.'

Had he gone mad or had she?

How could she have known it had been his? It made no sense, and he didn't want it to. The truth was nearly here and suddenly he didn't want to know.

'My father arranged…' It wasn't even been an adoption and her mind begged for a different word. 'My father facilitated…' And she searched for words that were kinder, tried to minimise even then what her father had done, but Nico did not wait for her to find the right words. Nico got straight to the brutal point.

'He sold me.'

'No.' It was too hard, even now, to face. 'A couple, your parents, wanted you. He arranged your birth certificate…'

'He sold me.'

'It wasn't like that...' She started to crumple, for she had seen the fees. She watched as he dressed, could feel the anger, the contempt, the rage that was building and would soon explode. She pulled the sheet around herself, wrapped it around her and held it tight as he demanded that she be honest. 'Yes,' she sobbed, 'yes.' She covered her face. 'Yes, he sold you.'

It was true, and now he knew it, and he knew too why he didn't belong—his father had swanned in and bought him, thought a baby was his God-given right. His father had taken him from his parents and he was taking from him now, because how could they come back from this?

'There's something else...'

Now, please now, silently he pleaded to a mind that was racing. Tell me I have a son, that I do have a family, a real one. Adrenaline coursed and he begged for reprieve, his head felt as if it were splintering. He could see her on the bed and he wanted to go back in there; he did not want it to be true. He wanted her and he wanted Leo, he wanted the family he had never been allowed to have.

'You have a brother.' Her words came like aftershocks, each one more violent than the last. He was pulling on his clothes and still the earth was moving. 'A twin.'

And he wanted it to stop, his anger taking aim, loss sweeping in, because always you lost, in love you lost.

'I should have told you!' she attempted. 'I wanted to.'

'There are so many things you haven't told me,' Nico shouted. 'So many things that I had every right to know.' He stood there, her accuser, and she sat guilty with shame but confused by his next question. 'Say it.'

'Say what?'

'Oh, please…' He could not believe that she didn't know what he was referring to. 'When are you going to tell me? Through a lawyer? Perhaps your father could draft the letter and tell me what I have to pay, in cash this time, because he's already taken everything else.'

She knew then he was talking about Leo as he raged on. 'When I came to your door, when I brought you here.' Nico's anger was growing now. 'Still you said nothing and now, even now, you sit there are refuse to tell me the truth!'

'Tell you!' It was Connie who was shouting now, Connie sitting there with anger growing inside her. 'We both know that it's eight o'clock.'

'What are you talking about?

'There's a clock by this bed and we can both see it, so why would you ask me the time? Do you want to split hairs? Do you want to say if it's a.m. or p.m.— when we both know?'

'I'm talking about Leo,' Nico roared. 'I'm talking about my son!'

'Your son,' Connie said. 'I am supposed to formally say it? What, will you demand DNA?' She could not match his anger but still hers was growing. Indignantly she ripped the sheet around her and stood, looked into his eyes and wanted to slap him. 'How dare you doubt me in this,' Connie sneered. She the injured party now. 'How dare you stand there and demand that I say that Leo is your son? I was a virgin, Nico, I had slept only with you and I have loved only you…' She stopped then because love did not count with him, love was the thing he did not want. Clearly did not want it, for he was walking out the door. 'Where are you going?' She had thought he'd want more answers, that he'd demand every detail, but realisation dawned and she ran at him and tried to halt him.

'Where do you think?'

She grabbed at his arm, but he flicked her off, and there was nothing, nothing that would stop him.

She watched as he charged from the house, heard a car screech from the driveway and gun down the hill, and he left her in chaos behind.

She wanted to ring her father, to warn him, to hate him.

To stop Nico, not just for her father's sake but to prevent what Nico would surely do.

CHAPTER SIXTEEN

HE WOULD kill him.

He would find where he lived and would go there.

Nico sped the car through the quiet morning, chewing up the miles with rage. He screeched to a halt at the toll barrier, blasting his horn impatiently for the watchman to lift it, ready to spring out and raise the thing himself. There was nothing on his mind but revenge, certainly no thought of consequences.

And the consequences for Connie were more than she could idly wait to unfold.

She rang her parents, desperate when they wouldn't answer, knowing they would now be on their morning walk, appalled at what they would come home to.

'He's fine!' Despina saw her anguish when, having quickly dressed, she fled to the old woman's door.

But it wasn't Leo she feared for.

She held him close, inhaled his delicious scent, and she was scared for her father and scared for Leo's father, too.

'Can you take me to my parents'?' Paulo came out

from a room at the sound of her anguish. 'Please…' she
sobbed. 'Nico is on his way there now.'

Paulo's car was no match for Nico's. It was small,
ancient, and Paulo wasn't up for a car chase. He am-
bled along the roads, even when she begged him to go
faster, but they had Leo in the car, Paulo pointed out,
and no car seat…and she looked at her baby and had
to bite her lip in frustration as Despina attempted to
reassure her.

'He's a good man,' Despina soothed.

He was a good man, a just man, Connie knew that,
but a terrible injustice had been done to him and when
Paulo asked at the road toll if they had seen him, a man
in silver sports car, her heart sank further. They were
told how he had been, angry and blasting his horn then
driving off as if the devil had been chasing him.

Paulo knew Xanos well and did not need directions,
but as they turned at the market square into her street
and drove up the hill, she was petrified what she might
see. She braced herself for a police car or for neighbours
on the street, for Nico's sleek sports car, but there was
nothing, no sign of Nico, or that he had even been here.
She asked Despina to wait with Leo as she ran up to
her front door, hammering on it, frustrated at the long
wait for her father to open it.

Slowly he did so and frowned at the sight of his es-
tranged daughter and then behind to where Despina
stood, holding his grandson.

'I don't take in beggars.' He went to close the door

and, Connie realised Nico didn't need to do it, she could quite happily have killed him herself.

'That's your grandson.' She barged in, powered on her own anger, proud, so proud to say it, for the truth to be known. 'His father is Nico Eliades.' And she watched her father's hand reach to his chest and she shook her head, for she would not let him manipulate her, would not let him hide behind a bedroom door with a nurse standing guard. 'He knows,' Connie said. 'He knows what you did and he's on his way here.' And she told him to get up when he fell to the floor. She told him to grow up when he begged out excuses and she told him to give her his office keys, to face Nico when he arrived and give him what he deserved.

His identity.

CHAPTER SEVENTEEN

Nico had screeched to a halt at the toll barrier, blasting his horn impatiently for the watchman to lift it, ready to spring out and raise the thing himself, and the wait did not calm him, the pendulum did not swing backwards. It just surged higher towards hatred, to filth, to violence, and the rule would be broken, Nico knew as his car swept into town, for this time the pendulum would never swing back.

No one would give him the address of Constantine's parents. As he stopped his car and demanded to know, people shrugged and walked on.

Why would they give directions? Nico realised. Who would give directions to a man raging? He stopped the car and forced himself to think.

She had lived near the taverna, Constantine had told him that, but he could not knock on every door. Someone would warn the bastard, or ring the police. Instead, he would go to the taverna and get directions. He would not get Charlotte involved with this.

And he forced himself calm, to appear just another

customer, and this time he did not take his coffee outside but drank it at the bar and chatted to the owner as
he looked through the menu, saw hot peppered calamari and wished, how he wished, that he had tasted it
with her. He wished they had bought it from here and
then sat on the beach as young lovers rather than the
nightmare that things were now.

Then he caught his reflection in the mirror, saw eyes
that were his, that were surely the same as his twin's,
and eyes, too, that were Leo's and Constantine was
right—she should not have had to say.

He did not need to be told that Leo was his son.

Which meant he was a father. And even if his mind
screamed for revenge, there was part of his mind that
was stronger, that waited, that paused as he drank his
coffee and, despite the hour, accepted the ouzo. He
tasted the anise on his lips and his mind went to his
twin.

He did not recoil at the thought now. At some level
he had always known, had recognised the face in the
mirror in a way that confused—and the jolt of surprise
he had felt when he had seen Leo had not been a father's normal reaction to his son.

Was that how he had looked?

He wanted names.

He wanted dates.

He wanted details.

A word to the owner and he had the address that
would take him to them. Nico paid and left and walked
past the beach where he would have held her, had he

been allowed to have his life, and to the bush where first he would have kissed her. Then he looked up at the hill behind her home, where his car would have taken her, and what they had found that night was how it should have been—for it would have been *their* wedding night, Nico realised, feeling a fresh surge of anger towards the man who had stolen from him so many things.

He pounded on the door, but it was she who opened it.

Dressed in the same dress she had worn last night, but dishevelled now, and he could see that she had been crying, hear the shouts and protests coming from behind her, telling her to close the door, not let him in. But she stood there, holding it open, and he looked down at her nervous, brave but somehow *still* trusting face, and he felt like he would had he loved her.

'Here.' She handed him that which should never have been taken. He looked at the names for a long moment, found Alexandros Kargas, who had been born on the same day as him, and found out, too, the names of his parents. A piece of his own jigsaw slotted in easily.

'It's my grandfather's home that I purchased...' Nico looked at his mother's maiden name. 'I am almost sure of it.' And hard as it might be, he was sure of one other thing as he looked back at Constantine—he had promised he would never hurt her.

'Can I come in?'

She hadn't expected him to ask, more that he would barge in, that there would be chaos, only Nico was deathly calm as he walked into the lounge. It was her father who leapt from his chair angry and confrontational, hurling his defence.

'I did the right thing by you,' was his uninvited response, for Nico had not said a word. 'Your mother was a hooker, a drunk. You would have had nothing had you stayed with her.'

'So I should thank you?' Nico's lips were white. With once sentence he silenced the man. 'And my father?' he demanded. 'What do you know about my father and brother?'

'They lived in the south. Your father was dirt poor, a brute who kicked you mom out. Should I have sent you back to him?'

And Connie learnt alongside him that his twin had long since left Xanos and his father had been dead for years.

'I did you a favour,' her father attempted, and she felt Nico tense, thought now the explosion would come, but still he stood there, told himself he fought only with equals, that a fist to an old man did not count and he would not break his code for a man so much beneath him. So instead he used words.

'Never say you did me a favour, never try to justify what you have done,' Nico said. 'You sold me, the same way you sold your daughter. What lies and deals did Dimitri threaten to expose if you did not use your daughter to cover for his son?' He watched her father grow pale as secrets were exposed and he clutched his hands to his chest, but it didn't wash with Nico. 'I am through speaking with you.' He turned to Constantine, who stood in the middle, saw her tears, her pain, and just wanted her out of there, 'Come with me,' he said, because he wanted her home.

'Talk to him, Connie,' her mother pleaded. 'Tell him how bad things will be for us if this ever gets out, tell him how bad things will look for his own son. Please, Connie…'

'It's Constantine,' she corrected, because that was how he had found her. 'And don't try to use Leo to sway things. Nico will do what he feels he must, and I will support him.'

Paulo and Despina were waiting outside and, though they promised they would take care of her son, Nico thanked them instead and told Connie to bring him. She walked, carrying her son, through the streets and the life that had been denied them, but somehow they had found this life anyway.

'What will you do?' She was still worried for her father.

'I will look for my brother.'

'I'll help you to find him.' But he knew that was not all she had been asking and she was brave enough to voice it. 'I cannot ask you to forgive my father when I don't think I ever will be able to…' She started to cry, because they had done things so terrible to the man she loved yet still they were her parents.

'One day you will forgive.' He took a deep breath. 'As one day I hope I can forgive the people who I call my parents. I give you my word, I will never make you choose…' She started to cry some more, but with a weak stream of relief, for it sounded as if there might be a future, but it all seemed too big. He held her in his arms, their son between them, and he was stronger.

So strong that he took the son he had feared loving and for the first time held him in his arms, felt the fear that came when you loved, but understood now the reward of it.

'I came here to kill him, Constantine. I drove into town and I was raging…' She knew that, had seen him leave, had spoken to the toll man, but she listened as he held her and breathed in every word he spoke.

'I went to the taverna, to our taverna.' And though they had never set foot in it together, as she looked up, her eyes told him she understood. 'I walked past our places, the beach where we ate, to the bush where we kissed, and then I walked to your door to face your father… That should have been how it was,' Nico said. 'Had I lived here in Xanos, I would be asking him for your hand, you would have been my bride a long time ago, which should make me hate him even more.' But walking that route, Nico had realised love was bigger, that somehow they were so meant to be, love had assured this moment. He knew that by hurting others he would hurt her, too, and he always kept his promise. 'It is a measure of how much I care for you and Leo that I will not destroy him.' And she started to cry again, only not with relief, because she knew how impossible those words she craved were for him—could see why he had not wanted love, for so many times it had been taken from him.

'Tell me…' she said, because she needed to hear those words. 'Tell me you love me.'

'I just did, I told you how much I care. Why make me say it? We both know…' And then he took a breath and said the words he never had before and had never thought that he would. 'I love you.' He gave her a smile and one that was for only her, and he made her laugh on a day she had thought she never would, because, as he told her, there was also some good news.

'We get,' Nico whispered, 'another wedding night, another night where you are my bride.'

EPILOGUE

Nothing could have prepared him for the impact of the telephone call.

Home, after a busy week of work, all Nico had intended was to take off his suit and join his new wife by the pool. It had been the simplest of weddings. The families were still too bruised for celebration, but slowly they were healing. With Charlotte as organizer and photographer, and Despina and Paulo as witnesses, they had married and returned to their hotel room for the second time, but legally now as husband and wife.

And Nico was happier than he had ever been, loved nothing more than to come home to his wife and to play with their chubby son, because finally he knew what evenings and weekends really were for.

Xanos was home.

He had been right. The house deeds showed that this had been his grandfather's home and now, years later, by universal inheritance it was his. The jigsaw that hung on the wall was his grandfather's artwork—a painting, Nico was sure, of himself and his brother, but unlike the jigsaw there were so many pieces missing. His search for Alexandros Kargas was proving fruitless. There were so many with that name. And then came the call.

'Can't it wait till Monday?' Constantine grumbled, as he suspended their kiss and answered the phone.

'Two minutes,' Nico said, 'then I will turn the phone off.'

It was longer than two minutes.

A lot longer.

Constantine watched as the sun lowered, the lengthening shadows creeping over her, and looked at Leo who was now drooping. She should bathe him and change him, but as she walked up the steps his head rested heavily on her shoulders and not only did she not have the heart to wake him for a bath, she wanted to be with Nico. She slipped Leo into his cot, changed his nappy as he slept, then covered him to the shoulders with cool gauze. As she stared down at her son, her eyes filled with tears and Constantine took a few calming breaths, somehow knowing that the news Nico had sought for so long had finally come.

As she walked into the living room, Nico stood in silence, staring at the jigsaw that was framed on the wall, and it was clear there was a conversation to be had.

She crossed the room and looked at the image with him. Still, they were searching for Roula, his mother, and they could not work out if Nico and his twin had ever lived in this home or had been, more likely from what the neighbours said, painted from his grandfather's imagination.

'I don't know if we'll get the land...' Nico said as she joined him, and his voice sounded normal. 'The owner still says that he is not willing to sell.'

'Oh.' She frowned because it surprised her that that was what was troubling him—she had thought he'd had news, big news, about his brother. She thought the endless searching had finally turned up something. It was only land they were talking about after all, and they had each other. Nico had long ago convinced her that she and Leo were all that mattered to him.

'The developer's name is Zander.' Nico said. 'Charlotte rang and said she had been speaking recently with Zander himself.' Constantine closed her eyes as Nico went and got the house deeds, as he turned to a signature that was so vital now. So vital that Nico ran his finger over the ink. 'Zander Kargas.'

'There could be many...' she attempted, but her heart, too, told her this was true. 'You need to speak to him,' Constantine said. 'Do you think...he knows...?'

'He knows,' Nico said. 'I am sure of it. Why else would he have sold me this home?'

'Because you paid a fortune.'

'No.' Nico shook his head. 'He knows who I am.' He handed her his phone, showed her the images he had just uploaded. It was bizarre: the man was the image of Nico, yet looked nothing like him—there was a savageness to him, a streetwise look that warned, from black eyes, not to approach. 'Our parents' home was the first that he bulldozed. I guess being left alone with that bastard has taken its toll. I just looked him up—he's ruthless, from what I've read about him. I don't think he sold me this house out of brotherly love.' He looked at Constantine. 'He lives in Australia, but he's talking about coming back to look at the development. I think he is hoping to shock me. He's playing games…'

'You don't know that.'

He did, but a wail from the bedroom meant he did not wait to explain why. Constantine followed as Nico went to tend to their son, her heart melting as she stood in the doorway and watched him settle Leo. He popped the baby's thumb back into his mouth and she watched as Nico looked for a moment into eyes that were his. She twisted inside for him, but tried not let him see it, could not imagine how it would be for him, to be about to meet a twin he had not known existed.

'Are you nervous about meeting him?' she asked when he joined her in the doorway.

'No.' Nico shook his head. 'It is too vital to be nervous.' And then he conceded, 'A bit.'

She thought of the future, of finding out the answers to all they were facing, but one thing was certain, not just for Nico but for her, too.

'Then I tell myself I have nothing to worry about.' Nico gave her that smile, the one that always melted her, the one that made her forget every problem. She understood exactly what he meant as he lowered his head to kiss her. 'After all, whatever the day brings, at night I come home to you.'

* * * * *

A sneaky peek at next month...

MODERN™

INTERNATIONAL AFFAIRS, SEDUCTION & PASSION GUARANTEED

My wish list for next month's titles...

In stores from 18th November 2011:

- [ ] Jewel in His Crown – Lynne Graham
- [ ] Once a Ferrara Wife... – Sarah Morgan
- [ ] In Bed with a Stranger – India Grey
- [ ] The Call of the Desert – Abby Green
- [ ] How to Win the Dating War – Aimee Carson

In stores from 2nd December 2011:

- [ ] The Man Every Woman Wants – Miranda Lee
- [ ] Not Fit for a King? – Jane Porter
- [ ] In a Storm of Scandal – Kim Lawrence
- [ ] Playing His Dangerous Game – Tina Duncan
- [ ] Acquired: The CEO's Small-Town Bride – Catherine Mann

Available at WHSmith, Tesco, Asda, Eason, Amazon and Apple

MILLS & BOON® Book Club

2 Free Books!

Get your free books now at
www.millsandboon.co.uk/freebookoffer

r fill in the form below and post it back to us

/Miss/Ms/Mr (please circle)

t Name

name

dress

Postcode

ail

nd this completed page to: Mills & Boon Book Club, Free Book
er, FREEPOST NAT 10298, Richmond, Surrey, TW9 1BR

ind out more at
w.millsandboon.co.uk/freebookoffer

Visit us Online

0611/P1ZEE

Have Your Say

You've just finished your book.
So what did you think?

We'd love to hear your thoughts on our
'Have your say' online panel
www.millsandboon.co.uk/haveyoursay

- Easy to use
- Short questionnaire
- Chance to win Mills & Boon®
  goodies

Tell us what you thought of this book now at
www.millsandboon.co.uk/haveyoursay

YOUR_SAY